# GHOST MAN

*"Dee! Come quickly."*

Dee ran over to the window and looked out. "Oh, my!" she gasped. Matthew Duncan, his black jacket flapping in the wind, stood at the base of the dogwood tree that was outside her window.

"Maybe he's just looking," Dee whispered, her heart pounding. "He might not really know you're here." Louisa and Dee leaned toward the window cautiously.

Matthew Duncan was beginning to climb the tree up to Dee's room!

They leapt back. Louisa covered her face with her trembling hands. "This is it. He's found me."

"Louisa, quick, disappear!" Dee urged her, and Louisa obeyed.

Desperately, Dee looked around the room. Her eyes fell upon the two *History of Misty Island* books. She grabbed both volumes from her desk and tucked them under her arm. Her hands shaking almost uncontrollably, she pushed up the window and hurled one, then the other heavy book at the man. Then, quickly, she slammed down the window and drew the curtains. Her heart was racing and her chest heaved with terror. The ghost was still climbing the tree and was about to reach the bedroom window. There was nothing she could do to stop him. . . .

HAUNTING WITH LOUISA

# The Mystery of Misty Island Inn

## Emily Cates

A BANTAM SKYLARK BOOK
NEW YORK · TORONTO · LONDON · SYDNEY · AUCKLAND

Many thanks to Suzanne Weyn
for developing the original concept for
Haunting with Louisa.

RL 4, 008–012

THE MYSTERY OF MISTY ISLAND INN
A Bantam Skylark Book / December 1990

ISBN 0-553-15858-9

Published simultaneously in the United States and Canada

PRINTED IN THE UNITED STATES OF AMERICA

OPM      0  9  8  7  6  5  4  3  2  1

# CHAPTER

# 1

Dee Forest reached one arm out from the warmth of her red and yellow patchwork quilt and grabbed the plaid flannel robe that lay on the end of her four-poster bed. Quick as a flash, she pulled it under the quilt. *It's freezing!* she thought. She let the robe warm a few minutes before squirming into it.

Only then was Dee ready to face another frosty cold morning at Misty Island Inn. Dee's Aunt Winnifred, who owned the place, believed in turning the heat down low at night. It not only saved fuel, but Aunt Win insisted the cold stimulated the brain. The only thought it stimulated in Dee was the wish that New England winters weren't so cold.

Dee reluctantly stepped out of bed, crossed the room, and pushed aside the heavy velvet curtains that were meant to keep the room warm. She looked out the window and smiled, glad to see that the heavy snow that had blanketed the island for over two weeks was finally melting. Small pockets of muddy brown now broke through the white of the silent snow. Spring was long overdue.

"Finally, some sign that winter won't last forever," came a warm voice directly behind Dee.

Dee turned quickly, but saw no one in the room!

Then, slowly, the air stirred. It became more and more turbulent, as if a warm wind were blowing in just one spot. The swirling currents of air began to pulse lightly. Soon, two periwinkle blue eyes were hovering, disembodied, in the air.

Dee stretched both hands toward the flowing air. It felt neither hot nor cold. The next thing she knew, a delicate white hand appeared and wrapped its fingers around her wrist. Another hand grabbed her other wrist and held on tight.

Seconds later, the full form of this strange apparition materialized. In front of Dee stood a girl her own age, thirteen. Long auburn curls framed the ghostly figure's perfect oval face. Her vibrant blue eyes contrasted sharply with the creamy pale color of her skin. She had a delicate upturned nose and a mouth that was perfectly shaped.

The ghost girl wore a long black pinafore over a high-collared, puffed-sleeve blouse. She might have stepped out of a scene from *Little Women* were it not for the pink high-topped sneakers peeking out from under the ruffled hem of her dress.

The ghost let go of Dee's wrists and staggered back a step. "I do not think I shall ever become accustomed to this appearing and disappearing business," she said breathlessly. "It does help to hold on to you, as you suggested yesterday, though I'm not at all sure why."

"I figured it might, Louisa," said Dee, calling her ghostly companion by name. "When you described how it feels to materialize, it reminded me of trying to get out of a boat and onto the dock when the boat is rocking up and down. I just thought it would be easier if you had someone on the dock to give you a hand. An anchor."

"I wonder if all ghosts have this difficulty," Louisa mused.

"Have you ever seen another ghost?" Dee asked.

Louisa's hand flew to her mouth in horror. "I never have. You know, I think I should die of fright if . . ." Louisa's voice trailed off, and she laughed sadly. "I suppose I don't have to worry about dying of anything anymore, do I?"

Dee didn't know what to say. Louisa often seemed to forget she was dead. The idea was still so new to her. Though a fire had destroyed the Lockwood home back in 1897, killing young Louisa Lockwood and her whole family, Louisa had no memory of the almost hundred years that had passed since then. The last thing she remembered was that she'd somehow become separated from her family as their spirits passed from this world. In a panic, she'd raced back to her family's home. But all she found there was a heap of ashes. Not knowing what to do, Louisa had sat down at the side of the road and wept. She cried and cried till there were no more tears. And then she fell into a long, deep sleep—a sleep that ended only six months ago, just as Dee had arrived on Misty Island.

At that time, Dee was moving into an upstairs room in Winnifred Forest's rambling old inn. There were almost no tourists on the resort island after Labor Day. It was only Dee and Aunt Win—or so Dee had thought.

Dee certainly hadn't been prepared to find a

ghost in her room. But once she had gotten to know Louisa, her initial terror gave way to sympathy for the ghost girl and her plight. Louisa was stranded between two worlds and all alone. Dee had just lost her mother in an auto accident, so she knew what it was like to feel lonely. Sympathy soon turned to friendship, and before Dee knew it, she and Louisa had become as close as sisters.

"I can't believe how cold it is in this place," Dee complained to her now.

Louisa shrugged, imitating the movement she'd learned from Dee. "It doesn't bother me. I don't feel hot or cold."

"Well, be glad of it," said Dee, rubbing her hands together briskly. "It's like an icebox in here."

Louisa's eyes lit up. "Do they still have iceboxes?"

"No," Dee answered. "What is an icebox, anyway? My mother always used to say it was as cold as an icebox when the boiler broke in our apartment building back in Cambridge. I never thought to ask her what it was."

"My mother had just gotten an icebox," Louisa said proudly. "We were one of the first families on Misty Island to have one. It was a big box with two chambers. You put a block of ice

5

in the bottom and that kept the food in the top from spoiling."

"Like a refrigerator without electricity, I guess," Dee suggested.

Louisa's face took on a puzzled expression. "Refriga—what?"

"It's a big box that keeps things cold by . . . well . . ." Dee hesitated. She wasn't really sure how it worked. "It's a modern icebox, I guess."

Suddenly there was a sharp rap on Dee's bedroom door. "Just a minute," Dee called nervously. She looked quickly to Louisa, but the ghost girl was already gone. "Come on in."

A woman of about sixty opened the door. She had bright orange hair and wore matching orange lipstick. In contrast, her clothing was quite sensible—a beige fisherman-knit sweater and green and blue plaid slacks. Dee could tell from the snow on her black boots that she'd already been outside.

"Good morning, Aunt Win," Dee said with a smile.

"Just wanted to ask if you had any plans for today," Winnifred inquired after giving her niece a hug and a kiss.

Dee shook her head.

"Good, because I'd like you to stick around. I have a wonderful surprise for you."

6

"You made your honey pancakes for breakfast," Dee guessed.

Aunt Win laughed the deep, husky laugh that Dee loved. "No, ma'am. This surprise is a whole lot better than that."

# CHAPTER
## 2

"Now will you tell me what the surprise is?" Dee pleaded as she stacked the dirty breakfast dishes onto a tray.

"Nope!" Aunt Win said mysteriously. "Just be here at eleven o'clock and we'll go get it together."

"Oh, come on, please tell me," Dee begged, her green eyes bright with excitement.

"It will be worth waiting for. That's all I have to say," Aunt Win teased. "What else are you going to do today?"

"Nothing. I'm just glad it's Saturday and there's no school."

A worried expression flickered across Win Forest's face. "You really don't like that school, do you?" she observed, carrying the dirty dishes from the dining room into the kitchen.

Dee followed and began helping her aunt stack the dishwasher. "I don't know," she said. "The school's okay, I guess. But the kids on the island have all known one another forever. They don't seem to want any new friends."

"Have you tried making the first move?" Aunt Win asked kindly.

Dee shrugged. She had a feeling her aunt already knew the answer to that question. Dee never invited any of the girls home after school. She never did anything on the weekends with anyone else.

Or so it seemed. In reality, of course, she had a constant companion—Louisa. And there was no one on Misty Island with whom she'd rather spend time.

"Be a good child and finish up in here, would you?" Aunt Win requested. "I have to make a phone call."

"Does the call have anything to do with the surprise?" Dee asked.

"Maybe," Aunt Win answered with a mischievous twinkle in her eyes.

Dee took a sponge and began wiping the kitchen counter. As she did, her thoughts drifted back to the bleak autumn day she had first arrived on Misty Island. The weather had been as gray and cloudy as her mood. That was back in September—just after her mother's death in the car accident.

Devastated by the tragedy, Mr. Forest had sent Dee to stay with Aunt Win while he made plans for their future. Dee had never felt so sad and lonely. Kindly Aunt Win had helped some. And so, of course, had Louisa.

Dee finished up in the kitchen and found her aunt at the desk in the front parlor. Winnifred was just hanging up the phone. "It's only the last week of March and folks are already calling for summer reservations," she said brightly. "I think we'll be full up all season."

No matter how hard she tried, Dee couldn't imagine the huge, creaky old inn packed with tourists. "I'm glad," she said, smiling affectionately at her aunt. "I guess I'll go for a walk until eleven o'clock," she said.

"All alone?" Aunt Win asked, frowning.

"I like to walk alone. Please don't worry about me. I'm okay," Dee assured her. "Really."

"All right," Aunt Win said, but she didn't sound convinced.

Dee got her down jacket from the hall closet and slipped into a pair of black boots with fleece lining. She took a red wool hat from her jacket pocket and covered her short blond hair with it. Then she stepped briskly out onto the front porch. "Louisa?" she whispered. "Are you there?"

There was a familiar stirring in the air, and soon Louisa reappeared. She wore no coat or hat, and her skirt flapped around her ankles in the cold New England wind. "I get cold just looking at you," Dee said.

"The cold doesn't disturb me," Louisa said. "Remember?"

"I know. But I still can't get used to the sight of you in the snow without a coat on."

A faraway look came into Louisa's eyes. "I used to hate winter because of having to bundle up. The last winter garment I owned was a heavy green wool cloak, which I despised. It was horribly heavy, and the hem dragged in the snow. I remember hoping I wouldn't have to wear that cloak next winter." A sigh escaped her lips. "Little did I know I would get my wish."

Dee put a comforting hand on Louisa's shoulder, but she didn't know what to say.

"I don't mean to be gloomy," Louisa went on. "I simply wish I were a live girl again, or that I was with my family. Hovering here, in between . . . it just doesn't feel right."

11

"That's why we're going to find your third relative," Dee said with as much assurance as she could muster.

"Do you truly think we can?" Louisa asked.

"Hey, we helped two already. We're halfway there," Dee reminded her.

"That's true," said Louisa. "When my mother came to me in the dream and said I had to help four relatives before I'd be allowed to rejoin the family, it sounded hopeless. But you helped me find and help the first two. Two more shouldn't be that hard. You're quite right. I shall try not to despair. We are, indeed, halfway there."

"Let's go into town now and look through the books in the library," Dee suggested. "I saw two books there last week—*The History of Misty Island,* volumes I and II. Maybe they'll help us figure out who some of your relatives married in the last hundred years. You must have some non-Lockwood kin on the island.

"It's worth a try," Louisa agreed.

The two girls headed down the snow-covered drive away from the inn. The melting snow made sloshing noises under Dee's feet. Louisa followed silently beside her.

At the end of the path was the main road, which wrapped around Misty Island and led into town. They ambled up the road, past the quiet church. The land to their right sloped down to a rocky beach, where the churning gray-blue ocean crashed against the muddy brown shoreline.

"Umm . . . Louisa," said Dee. "I think you'd better disappear. If someone in a car drove by and saw you walking around in that outfit, without a coat, we'd have some serious explaining to do."

"You are quite right," Louisa agreed, immediately starting to fade. "I forget sometimes."

To their left the land inclined gently. They passed a string of boarded-up guest houses and craft shops. Several homes, belonging to islanders, sat close to the road.

*Thwap!* A big, soft snowball skidded off the side of Dee's shoulder. It hit the road and bounced back up. With disbelieving eyes, Dee watched it roll across the road and settle on the other side. She ran over to retrieve it and laughed as she picked up a small rubber ball that had been covered with snow.

"Throw it back," a high-pitched young voice demanded. A blond boy of seven or eight was standing in the front yard of a gray, weatherbeaten house just off the road. "Throw it back," he repeated. "It's mine."

Dee brushed the remaining snow off the ball and hurled it as hard as she could. The boy jumped up and caught it, then came running toward her. "Just a few more throws," he pleaded. "There's no one to play with. I'm bored."

"Let's add a little excitement to this boy's day," Dee whispered to Louisa.

"What do you mean?" Louisa's disembodied voice replied.

"I have an idea," Dee said. "I'll show you." She held up her hands to the boy. "Let me see that ball."

When he tossed it to her, Dee pretended to examine the ball. "Just as I thought," she said. "This is a very special ball."

"Huh?" he asked, stopping at the edge of his yard.

"Yup. It's a boomerang ball," Dee told him, struggling to keep a straight face.

"What's that?" the boy asked skeptically.

"I'll show you," Dee said, stepping up from the road into his front yard. "Now watch. I'm going to throw the ball as hard as I can. It's going to stop in midair and then come flying back to me."

The boy laughed scornfully. "That's dumb. A ball can't do that."

"This one can," Dee insisted. "It will almost seem as if an invisible person had caught it and thrown it back," she added pointedly, wanting to be sure Louisa understood her part in the little trick. Dee took the ball with a flourish and tossed it across the yard. It went about thirty feet and then stopped, hovering un-naturally in midair before it came flying back to her.

"Wow!" cried the boy. "It really *is* a boomerang ball! Can I try?"

"Go ahead," Dee said, handing it to him.

The boy pulled his arm back and threw the ball. It sailed up into a high arc. Dee knew he had tossed it way over Louisa's head. But suddenly the ball stopped high in the sky. Again it hovered and then came sailing back to the boy.

"We can do this all day!" cried the boy.

"Uh, I'm afraid not. You see, the ball is only good for exactly ten throws," Dee bluffed. "Then it conks out."

The boy continued to throw the ball. Several of his throws were wild, and Dee was sure Louisa would miss them. But each time the ball stopped and then came back. Finally Dee called a halt to the game. "That's ten," she announced. "The ball has used up all its power."

15

Unconvinced, the boy tossed the ball again. This time it landed with a *plunk* in the wet snow. "Aw," he said, disappointed. But then his face brightened. "Wait till the other kids hear about this!"

"See, it wasn't such a boring day after all." Dee laughed. She waved good-bye to the boy and headed back down to the road, still smiling. The boy continued to wave until she rounded the bend and was out of sight.

"Well, that was fun," Louisa said, coming into view again. "I never used to be very good at playing ball," she admitted.

"You were catching that ball like a pro today."

Louisa smiled. "Yes. Well, being able to do this helps." And as she spoke, she floated up into the air until her sneakers were level with Dee's astonished gaze.

"Louisa, stop that!" Dee cried sharply, looking quickly up and down the road. "Someone is going to see you."

Laughing lightly, Louisa settled to the ground. "There's no one here," she said with a grin.

"You know," said Dee, "you always act so proper, but I think there's a bit of the devil in you."

Louisa's eyes went wide with horror.

"I don't mean a real devil," Dee hurriedly explained. "I mean you have a distinctly mischievous side—whether you want to admit it or not."

Louisa's smile returned. "Grandma Lockwood said I was the sassiest thing on Misty Island. But that was only because I preferred to collect shells and go fishing rather than learn to knit and sew. Compared to you, I was a very proper girl."

"Compared to me!" Dee exclaimed, pretending to be offended. "What do I do?"

"Where shall I begin?" Louisa laughed as they continued down the icy road, past another guest house boarded up for the winter. "You have short hair like a boy's, you wear trousers, and you even rouge your cheeks sometimes. Grandma Lockwood would faint if she—"

Suddenly Louisa stopped short. She clutched Dee's wrist with one hand while the other pointed shakily at the deserted guest house. "Oh, my soul!" she gasped. "It's him!"

Dee looked toward the house. At the window stood a tall, thin man, staring out at them. In the next second he stepped back into the shadows of the room and seemed to disappear. But not before Dee got a look at his unearthly pale face and glowing green eyes. "Who is he?" Dee asked Louisa urgently.

17

Louisa continued to stare at the vacant window. "It's him," she repeated. "He said he'd come to get me and he has. Matthew Duncan's come back from beyond the grave!"

# CHAPTER

# 3

"Louisa! Who's Matthew Duncan?" Dee asked. "And why has he come for you?"

Louisa's voice was filled with panic. "I thought I was safe from him. But his ghost has come to hurt me. He mustn't find me!" Louisa covered her face with her hands. Then, still trembling with fright, she disappeared without another word.

"Louisa? Louisa?" called Dee. "Come back!" There was no reply.

Her heart pounding, Dee approached the guest house. It was one of the smaller houses on Misty Island, probably with no more than four or five guest rooms. She stepped up onto the wooden porch. The wet boards creaked under her feet. She heard the distant drone of a snow-mobile. Other than that, there was an eerie silence.

A dull thud made her heart leap. She whirled around, only to see that a clump of snow had come loose from the roof and slid down onto the porch steps.

With a small sigh of relief, Dee stepped up to the front window. She wiped away the dirt and frost and peered through the clear circle. The room looked empty and still. Heavy canvas tarps were thrown over the furniture. A large rug had been rolled up and laid across two covered chairs. There was no sign of man—or ghost.

Cautiously, Dee walked around to the back. Her boots sank into the soft snow, and then farther into the mud below it. Just taking a step was difficult. She suddenly felt foolish for being so scared.

Making her way slowly to the back, she peeked in the porch window. Through the lace curtains, she saw the kitchen, quiet and undisturbed.

Then another sound made Dee jump. Alert, she listened. Was it more snow shifting?

There it was again! The same small sound. Dee's eyes darted to the corner of the building and she gasped out loud.

Before her stood the man from the window.

His skin was whiter than any she'd ever seen. He had high, sharp cheekbones and a long nose. His lips were so thin they hardly seemed to be there at all. His pale, watery green eyes were fixed on her intently.

Dee opened her mouth to scream, but her voice stuck in her throat. Filled with an overwhelming terror, she bolted off the far side of the porch. Without looking back, she ran up toward the road. She was almost there when she slid on a muddy patch. *Oooph!* She hit the ground hard.

She looked back and saw the man coming up behind her. His face was expressionless, except for those burning, red-rimmed eyes. His shapeless black suit jacket flapped behind him in the breeze.

Dee scrambled onto her feet and raced out onto the road. She didn't stop running till the inn was in sight. She glanced back quickly over her shoulder. The man was gone.

Her heart pounding against her chest like a jackhammer, Dee stopped to catch her breath. Only then did she start thinking clearly. She closed her eyes for a minute, and a perfect picture of her pursuer flashed across her mind. He hadn't been wearing a coat—or a hat, or boots. Like Louisa, he didn't seem to mind the cold. And his worn black jacket had no definite style. It could have been from any time. It could have been from Louisa's time. Dee drew in a sharp, cold breath. The man was a ghost!

Dee hurried toward the inn, checking again to be sure there was no one behind her. Her mind was busy, playing the scene at the guest house over and over, trying to make sense of it.

As she walked, she was aware that the sun was rapidly disappearing. The sky was growing thick with heavy, gray clouds. An eerie lavender-and-yellow-streaked light filtered through the clouds. Dee also noted that the waves were high. They were cresting and breaking out in the middle of the ocean. Her stay at Misty Island had taught her that these were all signs of an approaching storm.

She quickened her pace and was soon walking up the long gravel drive to the inn. She hoped Louisa had fled back to Dee's room and would be waiting for her there.

"There you are, Dee!" Aunt Win called from the porch. "I've been waiting for you. Come on. It's surprise time."

The surprise! Dee had forgotten all about it.

Aunt Win was wearing her blue pea coat and yellow boots. Without another word, she headed for the topless Jeep that stood in the drive. The top was buried somewhere in the tool shed. Hearty Aunt Win couldn't be bothered with it. She enjoyed a brisk ride in the open Jeep even in the worst weather. It was all part of her New England cold-stimulates-the-brain approach to good health.

Dee reluctantly joined her aunt at the Jeep. "Can't the surprise wait a little while longer?" she asked.

Aunt Win frowned. "What's the matter, Dee? You look as though you've seen a ghost."

For a moment, Dee considered telling Aunt Win about the man at the guest house. But how could she do that without explaining all about Louisa? And if she told Aunt Win she really *had* seen a ghost, her no-nonsense aunt would surely think she had lost her senses.

"I'm all right," Dee said. She showed Aunt Win the wet, muddy patch on the seat of her jeans where she'd fallen. "I fell, that's all."

"Anything hurt?" Aunt Win asked.

"No. I just want to go upstairs and change."

"All right," Aunt Win agreed. "But hurry. I don't want to keep the surprise waiting. Not with this storm coming."

Dee bounded into the house and up the stairs to the second floor. "Louisa?" she called, flinging open her bedroom door. "It's me. Are you in here? Are you all right?"

Dee waited. No Louisa. Then she heard a sound. It was coming from inside her closet. Someone was in there!

Dee barely dared to breathe as she backed up slowly toward the bedroom door. She was sure it was the ghost man. He must have followed Louisa home.

Dee was almost to the door. Just a few more steps.

Suddenly the closet door flew open. Dee fell back against the wall terrified. *Aaaaaiiiahhhh!* she screamed.

# CHAPTER

# 4

"Oh, my gosh, Louisa!" Dee gasped, her face almost as white as the ghost girl's. "What are you doing in the closet?"

"I have to hide. I don't think being invisible is enough. Matthew Duncan is a ghost, after all. He can probably see me even when I'm invisible." As she spoke, Louisa's eyes scanned the room rapidly, as if she expected the man to appear at any moment and from any direction.

"Who *is* this Matthew Duncan, Louisa? You still haven't told me. And what does he want from *you*?"

Just then Dee heard the sound of Aunt Win clamoring up the stairs. "Dee!" she called frantically. "Are you all right?"

Dee looked at Louisa quickly. "Don't disappear, okay?" she whispered, hurrying to the head of the stairs. "I'm fine," she called down to her aunt.

"I heard a scream!"

"Uh . . . sorry, I didn't mean to scare you. I . . . uh, just saw a mouse in my room. It startled me."

Aunt Win rolled her eyes. "That bloodcurdling shriek over a little field mouse? Really, Dee."

"Sorry," Dee repeated. "I guess I'm not exactly a real country girl yet."

"Come on, or we'll be late," Aunt Win urged.

Dee stepped back out of her aunt's view and turned to Louisa, who was cowering behind the bedroom door. She'd never seen her friend so upset. "Tell me, quickly, what's this all about?" she whispered.

"That man," Louisa began. "He swore he'd—"

"What's the holdup?" Aunt Win yelled impatiently.

"One sec," Dee called back. "He swore what?" she asked Louisa.

"If you're not down here in one minute, I'm leaving without you, Dee," Aunt Win hollered up the stairs. "I have to go whether you come or not!"

26

Dee was tempted to let Aunt Win go without her, but she didn't want to hurt her feelings. "Just stay invisible," she told Louisa, "and . . . I don't know . . . lock the door till I come back."

"Lock the door?" said Louisa. "That won't help."

Dee heard Aunt Win start up the engine.

"I'm sorry. I've got to go," said Dee. "But I'll come right back as soon as I can. I promise."

Aunt Win honked the horn to give Dee one last chance to join her.

"I'll be back," Dee repeated as she hurried down the stairs. "Just sit tight." She hesitated on the steps. "Everything will be okay," she said, hoping she was telling the truth.

"Sorry to rush you, dear, but we just have to leave," Aunt Win apologized when Dee joined her in the Jeep. "This surprise is on a definite time schedule."

"It's okay. I didn't mean to take so long," said Dee as they zoomed down the curving road that led to town. Dee could never get used to her aunt's breakneck style of driving. Aunt Win knew the Misty Island roads inside out and could anticipate every turn almost without thinking.

Soon they were passing through the heart of

town. Most of the shops were closed for the winter. Only the Misty Island Cafe and Clam Bar, the general store, Dodge's Fish Market, the post office, and a few other places stayed open all year for the islanders.

Aunt Win turned the Jeep onto a wide, sloping street that led to the harbor and ferry landing. Since they lived on an island, many things had to be brought over by boat. The main passengers on the ferry were truck drivers and their trucks filled with food, mail, medicine, gasoline, and other goods from the mainland. Dee could see the ferry about a half mile out at sea. Big as it was, it was rocking from side to side in the towering waves.

"Are we expecting someone on the ferry?" Dee asked.

"Yes, indeed," Aunt Win replied, hopping out of the Jeep. Dee followed her down to the dock, where several islanders were already waiting to meet the ferry. Mr. James, the postmaster, was there in his official truck to pick up the mail. "There's Mrs. Mason," said Aunt Win, pointing to a woman near the edge of the pier. "I want to talk to her about the next town council meeting. I'll be right back."

Aunt Win left Dee standing alone, watching the white gulls battle the air currents as they

28

followed the ferry into the harbor. It was a sight that usually made her feel very peaceful and content. But not today. She was still too frightened by the thought of Matthew Duncan. The image of his ghostly green eyes wouldn't leave her.

She hoped Louisa was all right. She wished the surprise would hurry and arrive. All she could think of was getting back home to Louisa. She'd never seen her friend so frightened. Why would anyone want to harm her? It didn't make any sense.

"Hi," came a voice behind her. Dee jumped. It was Nicky Dodge. "Sorry," he said, his hands jammed into his green down jacket. "I didn't mean to scare you."

"That's okay," Dee said with a smile. Nicky was two years ahead of her in school, but she knew him because he worked with his father at Dodge's Fish Market. Dee thought he was very good-looking, with his curly brown hair and lively blue eyes. Although she always felt shy and awkward when she spoke to him, she liked his easy, down-to-earth manner—and his adorable smile. "What are you doing here?" she asked.

"I'm with my dad," he said with just a hint of the accent that identified him as an islander.

He nodded toward his father, a broad-shouldered man who stood talking to Mr. James. "We're meeting my grandfather. He's coming back from the mainland with materials we need to put in some new display cases. How about you?"

"I don't know," Dee replied. "Aunt Win says we're waiting for a surprise."

"Sounds exciting," he commented, flashing the wide grin that always made Dee blush.

"Aunt Win sure seems excited about it," she said.

The ferry whistle blasted twice as the boat banged lightly against the pier. "Got to go," said Nicky, looking toward his father, who was motioning him over. "I'll see you around."

"I hope so," said Dee, waving to him as he ran off.

Deckhands in heavy orange coveralls jumped off the ferry and began securing it to the dock. "This is it. This is it," said Aunt Win, hurrying over. "Come on."

Dee followed Aunt Win right up to the ferry. The gate opened and a procession of trucks rolled out of the lower deck. "Which truck has the surprise?" Dee asked, studying each one as it pulled out.

"None of them," said Aunt Win. She leaned

in close to Dee and pointed. "There's your surprise!"

Walking off the ferry to the side of the trucks was a lanky man with thinning blond hair. He carried a large brown suitcase and had a camping pack slung over his shoulder. He was looking around as if he wasn't sure which way to go.

*"Daddy!"* Dee cried, running toward him.

Dee's father dropped the suitcase when he saw her. She ran right into his outstretched arms and hugged him tight. She'd known she missed him, but she hadn't realized just how much until this moment. To her surprise and slight embarrassment, hot tears of joy filled her eyes.

"Why the tears, sweetheart?" her father asked.

"I guess I'm just so happy to see you," Dee answered, brushing the tears away. "Why didn't you tell me you were coming?"

"I wasn't sure until yesterday I could actually make it. I didn't want to say I was coming and then have to cancel."

"I can't believe you're really here. I'm so happy!" She hugged him again, squeezing as hard as she could.

Suddenly Dee was struck with a troubling thought. Had her father come to take her home?

Months ago, that was all she'd dreamed of. But she couldn't leave now. Not when Louisa was in danger. "Why are you here?" she asked seriously.

"I wanted to spend some time with you. I missed you. I took a leave of absence from work. I need a rest, and there's no reason I can't rest here on Misty Island."

"You mean you're staying? I don't believe it! This is too great!"

Just then Aunt Win joined them, throwing her sturdy arms around Dee's father. "John Forest, you're as handsome as ever," she cried. "You are a sight for sore eyes. It seems like ages since we've seen each other."

"It has been too long, Win," he replied. "But there's no reason we can't make up for lost time now."

"I'm so pleased," said Aunt Win. "Now first let's get you home and fed. That ferry ride must have been something. I can't remember the last time we've had such rough waters here."

"You're telling me," Dee's father said. "The rocking of that ferry was making me seasick. And there's no heater on that thing, either."

"The winter ferry is really just set up for trucks," said Aunt Win. "The drivers don't even leave their warm cabs."

"Excuse me," said a attractive-looking woman, coming up beside them. "Do you know where I could get a taxi?"

"No taxis this time of year," Aunt Win answered. "Where are you going?"

"I'm not sure. I was hoping the driver could take me to a hotel," the woman answered, tucking a piece of her shoulder-length brown hair back into her rose-colored wool hat.

Flushing slightly, Mr. Forest introduced her as Eva Barlow. "Eva and I met on the ferry," he explained to Dee and Win. Then, turning back to Eva, he said, "You should have told me you needed a place. Aunt Winnifred here runs the best inn on Misty Island."

"Not only is it the best," added Aunt Win with a chuckle. "It's also one of only two inns open all-year round. And the other one, the Seagull Inn, is a terrible shambles of a place."

"So your choices are Misty Island Inn, Misty Island Inn, or Misty Island Inn," teased Dee's father.

"I guess I want to go to Misty Island Inn, then," said Eva, her brown eyes smiling.

"Excellent choice," Mr. Forest said. "We just happen to be going that way ourselves. Can we give you a lift?"

"That would be delightful," she said.

Dee looked at her father and noticed the merriment in his eyes. It was so good to see him smiling. Then she realized something else. Her father was flirting with this woman. She was sure of it. But even as she realized that this was something that upset her a bit, she suddenly had another disturbing thought—Louisa! For a few minutes she had forgotten all about her.

Thrilled as Dee was to see her father, all she wanted now was to get home. She couldn't enjoy her father's arrival until she knew her friend was safe. "Let's get going," she said to the group, trying not to sound too anxious.

"Yes, before this storm hits," Aunt Win agreed.

The four of them climbed into the Jeep, Dee's father and Aunt Win up front, Dee and Eva in back. Dee noticed that her father's new friend smelled of a warm, spicy perfume. She wore jeans and a denim jacket over a bulky brown turtleneck sweater. A person might consider her attractive—a person like her father.

Before starting the engine, Aunt Win honked her horn playfully at the Dodges. Nicky, his father, and his grandfather were lugging some wooden crates up the sloping drive. "How are

34

you doing, Jack Dodge, you old goat?" she called to a handsome man with a mane of flowing white hair.

"Just dandy, Winnie. When are you going to invite me over for some of your famous clam chowder?" he answered. Nicky, who was carrying the other end of the crate his grandfather held, looked up at Dee and smiled. She smiled back at him.

"I'll make a batch specially for you and give you a call," Aunt Win shouted, and then she stepped on the gas. Soon they were speeding around the curving road that led back to the inn. Dee smiled at the horrified expression on her father's face every time they careened around a turn. She was used to Aunt Win's driving by now.

Suddenly fat flakes of snow began to fall. "Almost there," Aunt Win shouted over the wind. "I knew this storm would be on us soon."

Just minutes later they were rumbling up the bumpy gravel path. The snow was falling heavily now, dusting their heads with a thick layer of white.

"I can't believe this weather," Dee's father said. "Isn't this supposed to be spring?"

"It's *supposed* to be, all right," Aunt Win admitted, hopping out of the Jeep.

"Hurry now. Let's get inside," she urged. "I made a special lunch."

Dee glanced anxiously up at her bedroom window. She had to get back there and make sure Louisa was all right.

# CHAPTER

# 5

Aunt Win held up the big steaming bowl and offered it first to their guest. "I remember that my nephew loves my candied yams. Hope you do, too."

"It all looks so good," Eva replied, gazing over the feast of turkey, yams, string beans, and cranberry sauce Aunt Win had set out.

"It smells as delicious as I remember," Dee's father said, heaping his plate with turkey. "You've even made oyster stuffing. Incredible!"

Aunt Win gave him an approving smile. Then she looked at Dee, who hadn't put a thing on her plate yet. "Dee, come on, eat," she said, passing her the platter of turkey.

Dee took a small slice of turkey, but let it sit

on her plate. She was much too worried to eat. Aunt Win had immediately put her to work setting the table when they came in, so she hadn't had a chance to check up on Louisa. She *had* to find out what was going on upstairs!

"May I please be excused?" Dee asked abruptly.

"But you haven't eaten," her father objected.

"Maybe it's just the excitement, but my stomach hurts a little," Dee said. She hated to leave him, but she *had* to get up to her room.

"It's probably from not eating," said Aunt Win. "Have a few bites. You'll feel better." Aunt Win continued to pass the food. Dee took the smallest amount possible and began shoveling it into her mouth.

"See, you were hungry," said Aunt Win. Then, turning to Eva, she asked, "What brings you to the island at this time of year? Are you visiting someone?"

"No, I don't know a soul on this island. It's your birds I've come to see," Eva answered. "You get some winter birds here that aren't found everywhere else. I'm an artist and I want to sketch them."

"That's fascinating," said Aunt Win. "Don't you think so, Dee?"

"Yes, yes, it is," Dee said, getting up from her chair. "I have to go lie down. Please excuse me."

"Can I get you anything?" Aunt Win asked with concern.

"No, I'll be okay," Dee said.

"Go ahead and rest, honey," her father said. "You do look a little out of sorts."

Dee nodded and hurried upstairs. Outside her room, she paused and took a deep breath. Then she opened the door a crack and peeked in. "Louisa?" she whispered.

"I'm here," came Louisa's disembodied voice. "What took you so long?"

"Sorry. I got back as soon as I could," Dee said, stepping into the room and shutting the door quickly behind her.

Louisa slowly became visible. She was sitting on the edge of Dee's bed, her hands squeezed tightly together on her lap. Dee turned her desk chair around and sat on it backward. "What *is* it, Louisa? What's going on? You've got to tell me everything. Otherwise, I won't be able to help you."

"It isn't a nice story," Louisa said, her voice trembling. "I've been thinking and thinking about it ever since I saw him. I can see all the faces again. I can feel the hatred."

"Hatred? Whose hatred? And who is *he*?"

Louisa nodded. "Yes, hatred. I've already told you that man is Matthew Duncan. He and his family used to live next door to us. The Duncans were a strange family, very quiet. They kept to themselves. Most of the people on the island disliked them, but my mother tried to be charitable. She sent over baked treats for their children and always greeted them respectfully.

"Then, last year—" Louisa interrupted herself and gave a sheepish smile. "Sorry, it still seems like last year to me. The year before our house burned, Mrs. Duncan came down with the smallpox. Then two of their three children got it. Matthew came begging my father for help since he was the only doctor on the island. He said he had no money to pay my father, but Papa never cared about money. The problem was that there *was* no medicine for smallpox."

"So what did your father do?"

"He went to see them, and tried to make them as comfortable as possible, but there really wasn't much he could do. Matthew Duncan didn't believe him, though. He thought my father wasn't giving them the medicine because he couldn't pay for it. No matter what my father said, he simply wouldn't believe that the medicine didn't exist."

"Then what happened?" asked Dee, leaning forward on the chair.

"Eliza—his wife—got weaker and weaker. She

finally died. Then the kids went, just a day apart from one another. Matthew simply couldn't bear it. He lost his senses, went completely mad."

"I can still see him pounding at our front door, his face red with rage, sweat streaming down his forehead. Only my mother and I were home at the time. He was screaming at us. Screaming that he'd get his revenge no matter how long it took. He upset my mother so much that he made her cry."

"That wasn't right," said Dee.

"I know, and as sorry as I felt for him, he made me angry. My mother was the only person who had been kind to his wife and children. I told him so, too. I yelled back at him. I told him to get off our porch immediately."

"Good for you."

"No, it wasn't so good for me," said Louisa seriously. "He began saying crazy things, that it had all been *my* fault, that *I* had given his wife the smallpox. He even accused me of hiding the medicine. He was just mad out of his mind. But he swore he would get me someday, make me pay for my sins."

"That's horrible," Dee whispered, shaking her head.

Louisa stared out the window for a long time.

The snow was falling heavily now. The bare branches of the dogwood tree outside the window were blanketed in crystal white. "Yes," Louisa agreed. "And now I can't help wondering if Matthew Duncan didn't set the fire that killed my family and me," she went on, not moving her eyes from the window.

Dee realized that Louisa's eyes were brimming with tears. "Louisa . . ." She wanted to say something, anything, to make Louisa feel better, but she couldn't find the words.

"And now he's come for me," Louisa said, still staring ahead. "Matthew Duncan's ghost has come for me."

"But why?" Dee asked. "What can he possibly want with you now?"

Louisa turned back to Dee, her lower lip trembling with fear. "I don't know. But you saw him. You saw how hateful he looks. Maybe he can take me to some terrible dark place, someplace where I'll never see the light again."

Louisa covered her face with her hands and wept. "I'm so scared, Dee. What if he takes me away? I'll have no hope of finding my other relatives then. And I'll never see Mother, Papa, and Edward again. I can't bear the thought. I just wouldn't be able to stand it." She began to weep again. "He's a mean man. Who knows what he'd do to me?" she sobbed.

Dee got up and sat on the bed beside Louisa. Tenderly, she put an arm around the ghost girl's quivering shoulders. Louisa felt so light, neither warm nor cold.

"I was frightened back then, but I had my mother and father. I always felt so safe with Papa. I knew he wouldn't let Matthew Duncan hurt me," she said, wiping her eyes. "But now . . . now they're both gone. I'm scared, Dee. There's no one to protect me anymore. I'm all alone."

"I won't let him hurt you," said Dee firmly.

"Thank you. But I don't see how you can possibly stop him."

Suddenly Dee had an idea. "If we can hurry up and help two more of your relatives before Matthew Duncan finds you, you can go back to your family. He won't be able to do a thing about it."

"It sounds like a fine plan, but I don't think we'll be able to find them quickly enough," Louisa answered.

"Come on," Dee said, "show some spirit." Then, just realizing what she'd said, she giggled.

Normally Louisa would have laughed at Dee's unintentional joke. But this time she sat glumly on the bed. A deep, despairing sigh escaped her lips. "Oh, Dee," she finally said. "I forgot to ask about your surprise."

Dee squeezed Louisa's hand. "It was the best surprise you can imagine. My father got some time off from work. He's going to stay here awhile."

Louisa smiled softly. "I'm so happy for you. I shouldn't be burdening you with my problems."

"It's okay, Louisa. I know how you feel. I saw that creepy Duncan guy, too. He chased me away from the guest house. I was snooping around after you disappeared, trying to figure out what was going on."

Louisa gasped. "Promise you won't go near him again. I'd never forgive myself if anything happened to you because of me."

"Don't worry," said Dee. "He's scary as anything. If I see him again, I'll run the other way. I will help you, though. You can count on me."

"I know I can," Louisa said. "Now please go back down and see your papa. I feel a little tired. All this worrying has worn me out."

"All right," Dee said quietly. She gave Louisa a hug and then went out into the hallway. She didn't hear anyone talking downstairs. Maybe Aunt Win had already shown her father to his room. She walked down the hall and noticed a door that had been left open a crack. Thinking it might be her father's room, she peeked in.

Instead of her father, she saw Eva sitting on the edge of the bed, talking on the phone to someone.

"Yes, I'll try," Dee heard Eva say. "The Misty Island Cafe and Clam Bar? I'm sure I'll be able to find it. This whole island is practically shut down. I'll do my best, but I can't promise you. Especially not with this snow falling. If I don't show up tonight, wait for me the same time tomorrow. No, don't call me here, whatever you do."

*That's very strange*, Dee thought, continuing down the hallway. Eva had said she didn't know anyone on Misty Island. Who could she be planning to meet? And why would she lie?

# CHAPTER

# 6

The snow had stopped by Sunday morning, having covered all the muddy slush with a fresh layer of white. Dee's father insisted that they go sledding together. Although she was worried about leaving Louisa, Dee was eager to spend the time with him.

The day passed quickly. They sledded and walked all the way to town, stopping for hot chocolate and sandwiches at the Misty Island Cafe and Clam Bar. They talked a little about Dee's mother and how much they both missed her.

It was a wonderful day. Dee would have been very happy if it weren't for the problem of Matthew Duncan. On the pretense of showing her father the library, she went and checked out the two books she had mentioned to Louisa— *The History of Misty Island*, volumes I and II. Maybe there would be something about Louisa's family in them.

"Dad," Dee said as they trudged back up the snowy road toward the inn. "What do you think of Eva?"

"I don't know," her father answered. "She seems nice."

"You like her, don't you?" said Dee, testing.

"What do you mean?"

"You know what I mean, Dad," Dee insisted. "You were looking at her with your eyes all flutterylike."

Her father laughed self-consciously. "Was I? How did I look?"

Dee opened her eyes wide and batted her lashes rapidly.

"Wow! I must have looked pretty strange then," he said with a laugh. "I'm surprised she didn't run right back onto the ferry."

"You're not answering my question," said Dee. "Do you like her?"

"She's very nice," he answered, his face growing serious.

"Then you *do* like her."

"Not in the way you mean, Dee," he replied.

47

"I loved your mother very much. I think it's going to be a long, long time before I feel the same way about anyone else. A long time. Maybe it will never happen again."

His voice caught in his throat and Dee felt his terrible sadness. She put her gloved hand in his, and they continued walking silently up the road. She had been leading up to telling him about Eva's mysterious phone conversation, but suddenly it didn't seem like the right time. It wasn't that important. It could wait.

Back at the inn, Aunt Win greeted them with mugs of mulled cider and sat them down to a dinner of baked ham, sweet potatoes, and string beans. When Dee asked where Eva was, Aunt Win said she didn't know. She'd gone out that afternoon and wasn't expected back until after supper.

"Probably out looking for birds," her father suggested as he sliced the ham.

"Probably," Dee replied flatly, a hint of skepticism in her voice. That woman just didn't seem like the bird-watching type to Dee. And didn't artists usually carry big satchels with their paints and brushes inside? Oh, well, she thought, maybe Eva's stuff was in her suitcase.

After dinner, Dee excused herself and brought the two library books up to her room. Louisa appeared as soon as she walked in. "Here, you take volume one," Dee said, tossing a book to Louisa. "I'll take the other one and we'll see if we can find anything about your family."

They lay down on Dee's bed, Louisa curling, ladylike, at the foot, Dee sprawled at a diagonal. They quickly paged through the books, scanning the type for any mention of the name Lockwood.

"Look! Here is a picture of me and my classmates," said Louisa excitedly. She showed Dee a faded photograph of a small wooden building. Ten children were lined up on its porch. There were four tall girls and one boy in the back and five shorter boys in front. "There I am," said Louisa, pointing to the old photo. She stood smiling at the camera in a white smock dress with puffed sleeves. Her hair was in curls, the breeze was tossing them around her shoulders. Her bright eyes sparkled with life. How pretty and happy she looked, Dee thought.

"That's Tobias Dodge." Louisa pointed to the tall boy in the back row. He wore a white shirt with no collar, and baggy pants held up by suspenders. His serious expression set off his straight mouth and strong jaw. The breeze blew the tangle of dark curls over his forehead. "Remember, I told you, that's the boy I liked so much."

"Wow!" cried Dee. "He looks exactly like Nicky Dodge. It's amazing—weird even."

"They're both quite good-looking," Louisa agreed wistfully.

"They sure are," Dee said, sighing.

They went back to their books. "Hey, take a look at this," said Dee a few minutes later, passing her book to Louisa. It was opened to a photo of a young man in a heavy pea coat who was standing proudly in front of a small skiff. "It says here that Nicky's grandfather—I guess that means Jack—won the Gold Carnegie Medal, the highest honor the Carnegie Hero Award Commission can give. It says he saved some survivors of a shipwreck by going out in his boat during a storm to pick them up. That was back in 1939."

"Yes, there have always been shipwrecks off this shore. It's so rocky and shallow at points," Louisa noted, handing the book back to Dee and picking up her own again. "This is so fascinating, reading about all the things that happened while I was asleep."

"Unfortunately, it's not helping us so far. Didn't you have any cousins or anything?"

"After my Uncle Thomas died, Aunt Rose

took the children with her to Boston. I don't see any mention of my second cousins here. Perhaps they left the island as well," Louisa replied.

Dee went back to reading. "Here's Mrs. Lockwood winning some flower show award. But we've already helped her and Harry."

Louisa looked over her shoulder at the picture of Mrs. Lockwood with her prize-winning orchids. "She was so pretty when she was young," Louisa observed. "But what a strange outfit." The picture had been taken in the fifties and Mrs. Lockwood wore a print dress with a flared skirt.

Dee yawned. "I'll have to finish this tomorrow," she said sleepily. "I'm ready to crash."

"What?" Louisa asked, alarmed.

"Not really crash. I mean go to sleep," Dee explained.

"Good night, then," said Louisa, fading away.

Dee put the books on her desk and got undressed. She pulled on her flowered nightgown, crawled under the cozy yellow and red quilt, and snapped off the light on her bedstand. As she was drifting off to sleep, she realized she'd forgotten to close the curtains. She looked at the moonbeam shining through her window, illuminating the open library book on her desk.

Dee's eyes grew wide when she saw one of the pages quietly flip over all by itself.

"Louisa?" she whispered.

"Yes, it's me," came Louisa's dreamy voice. "I can't seem to put this down."

"Oh," Dee murmured, before rolling over and dropping off to sleep.

# CHAPTER
# 7

The next morning Dee was awakened by the sound of howling wind. The branches of the dogwood lashed at her window as if trying to break the glass. Icy rain pelted the inn.

"April certainly is coming in like a lion," said Aunt Win, standing in her doorway. "I thought March was supposed to do that."

"Do I have to go to school today?" Dee moaned, trying to sound as pitiful as possible.

" 'Fraid so." Aunt Win laughed. "But I came up to tell you I'll drive you."

"That won't do much good, will it, Aunt Win?" Dee asked, trying to be tactful. "The Jeep still gets pretty wet on days like this."

"Oh, you know your father, Mr. Efficient," said Winnifred. "He dug out the top and put it on last night. I'll miss the fresh air. It stimulates the brain, you know."

"I know," Dee said, smiling. "Hey, something's different here this morning. I'm not freezing."

"We have a paying guest now," Aunt Win reminded her. "Guests don't always like to have their brains stimulated, so I turned up the heat a bit."

"It feels great," said Dee, hopping out of bed. Eva had come in handy for something, anyway. As soon as Aunt Win left, Dee called for Louisa and the ghost girl slowly appeared, yawning and stretching.

"I read both those books last night," she said, stifling another yawn. "They were fascinating, but there's nothing in them to help us."

"Want to come to school with me?" Dee asked, stepping into her jeans.

Louisa shook her head forcefully. "I'm staying right here. I can't risk Matthew Duncan seeing me."

"Maybe he's gone," Dee suggested. "We haven't seen him since Saturday. He's probably given up."

"I don't think so. A madman doesn't come

back from the dead and then simply give up. He's out there. I can almost sense his presence," Louisa said, looking nervously around the room as if expecting him to materialize right then and there.

"Okay, then. Stay here until I get back from school," said Dee, running a brush quickly through her hair before heading downstairs. Her father and Eva sat chatting at the dining-room table over the remains of a pancake breakfast.

"See any good birds yesterday?" Dee asked Eva as she poured herself some orange juice.

Eva looked at her blankly for a moment. "Oh, yes," she said. "This is a wonderful place for birds."

"Would you show me your drawings later?" asked Dee.

Eva shifted slightly in her chair. "I hate to show my work when it's still in the sketch stage. I'm funny that way. I only like people to see the finished product. I guess I'm a perfectionist or something."

*Or something*, Dee thought suspiciously. There was definitely something about Eva Barlow that didn't add up.

Dee was just finishing her breakfast when Aunt Win came out of the kitchen. "Let's go,"

Winnifred said, pulling on her green parka. "Take an umbrella from the hall. And this—" She handed Dee a brown paper lunch bag. "A turkey sandwich with cranberry sauce," she announced. "There was a lot left over from Saturday."

Dee smiled at her. "Thanks."

Together they left the inn, bowing their heads against the icy rain as they dashed to the Jeep. Dee silently thanked her father for putting the top on. In a few minutes they were roaring down the main road.

Normally Dee walked the half mile to school. There were so few year-rounders on Misty Island that there were only two schools. The one Dee attended, for grades one through eight, and the high school, just another half mile down the road.

Aunt Win dropped Dee off in front of the square brick building. There was a small traffic jam of four-wheel-drive Jeeps, vans, and flatbed pickups as well as regular cars dropping their passengers off. A yellow minibus pulled in. Every morning it picked up the few students who lived on the far side of the island.

Dee looked out the window and saw the kids hurrying into the building, their coats flapping and their umbrellas snapping inside out. "Thanks for the ride," she said, leaning over to give Aunt Win a quick kiss on her soft cheek.

Stepping out of the Jeep, Dee felt the stinging chill of the cold rain on her face. She put up her umbrella and was heading straight for the front steps when, suddenly, she heard a loud crash. She looked down and saw the shards of a clay flowerpot, clumps of potting soil, and a broken-stemmed orchid on the ground several feet away. Then a heavyset boy came sliding along the muddy ground right in front of her feet. His black-rimmed glasses slid another few feet beyond him.

Startled, Dee jumped back. She recognized the boy. It was Jerry Mason from the seventh grade. "Are you all—" she began.

"Ah, hah, jerky Jerry, tripped over his own feet," came the taunting voice of a stocky boy nearby. It was Larry Moss, another seventh-grader.

"You pushed me!" cried Jerry, climbing awkwardly to his feet. "And you broke my aunt's orchid."

"Oh, excuse us," snarled a tall, muscular boy beside Larry. Dee knew him because he was in her class. His name was Rob Thomas. "It's not every day I see a pansy with an orchid." Both boys broke out into loud, snorting laughter.

"Hey, why don't you leave him alone!" shouted Dee, picking up Jerry's dirty glasses.

"Who are you, his mommy?" challenged Larry.

"Why don't you two infants get lost," Dee snapped.

"Aw, little Jerry needs a girl to protect him," Rob sneered as the two boys stepped around Dee and Jerry and went into the school.

Jerry knelt over the broken pot, frantically trying to pat the dirt back around the fragile plant's roots. "My aunt is going to kill me," he muttered. "I begged her to let me have this orchid for part of my science project. I told her I'd be super careful with it."

Dee realized they were both getting drenched, but she bent down to help the boy pick up the pieces of the pot. She opened her knapsack and pulled out her lunch bag. Dumping the wax paper–wrapped sandwich into her pack, she handed the brown bag to Jerry. "You can put the orchid in this, but hurry before it gets too wet."

Jerry held the plant by its roots and eased it into the bag. Dee looked at the showy purple flower as he worked. Then it hit her.

58

"Did you say this is your aunt's flower?" she asked.

Jerry nodded. "She grows them in a greenhouse. I thought I'd do my project on—"

Dee cut him off. "Is your aunt Mrs. Lockwood, by any chance?" she asked excitedly.

# CHAPTER

## 8

Dee sat at her desk and watched the rain splash against the window while Mrs. Breyer tried to explain why the Spanish American War had been inevitable. Dee liked history, but she was too excited to pay attention. She had found him—a third relative of Louisa's. As far as Dee knew, there was only one woman who had a greenhouse on Misty Island—Mrs. Lockwood. Since Jerry was related to her, that meant he was also related to Louisa.

And if there ever was a boy who needed helping, it was Jerry Mason. All Dee had to do now was figure out what they could do for him.

She remembered Jerry from another time when some kids had been picking on him. Being picked on was probably a way of life for the poor guy. What did he need? More confidence? More friends? Karate lessons? A diet?

Dee knew two things for sure. First, she would have to get to know Jerry better. Second, Louisa would, too. It wouldn't do any good if Dee helped him. Louisa had to do it.

When three o'clock finally came, the kids formed little groups and left together. "Want to come down to the clam bar with us?" a girl named Helen asked as she and Dee headed out the door.

"Thanks, but I can't," Dee answered. "I have things to do at home."

"Okay," said Helen before running to catch up with her friends. Dee saw a couple of the girls look back at her. Helen shrugged at something they said. They were probably telling her not to bother, that Dee always kept to herself.

Dee frowned as she stood in front of school and waited for Jerry to come out. The rain had subsided to a slow drizzle, but she was getting a chill standing there. Where *was* that boy?

Dee recognized Mrs. Lockwood's old black Plymouth with its wide fins as soon as it turned into the drive and pulled up at the side entrance. "Hi, Mrs. Lockwood," she said, walking up to the car.

Mrs. Lockwood rolled down the window. A woman who looked like a much younger version of her was slouched in the passenger seat. "Hello, dear," Mrs. Lockwood greeted Dee fondly. "You haven't by any chance seen my nephew, Jerry?" she asked, smoothing a strand of her wavy brown hair. "My sister's car wouldn't start up in this rain, so I gave her a lift to pick him up."

Dee looked around. Still no Jerry. "I saw him this morning, but I haven't seen him since," she said.

"I guess he's gone on ahead," Mrs. Lockwood said, sighing. "Can I give *you* a lift?"

Dee was glad to accept. She couldn't wait to get home and share her discovery with Louisa. Quickly, she climbed into the backseat. "This is my sister, Hilary Mason," Mrs. Lockwood introduced her.

"Hi," said Dee. "I've seen Jerry around school, but I just really met him today." She debated telling them about the bullies, but decided against it. Jerry might not appreciate her interference. "Would it be all right if I came by to visit Jerry this afternoon?" Dee asked.

Mrs. Mason seemed surprised but pleased. "Why would you want to do that?" she asked. From her response, Dee could tell that Jerry wasn't exactly overloaded with friends.

"He seems like a nice kid," said Dee.

"Well, I'm sure he'd love to see you, but Jerry has an appointment with the dentist this afternoon. How about tomorrow?"

"Jerry was planning to come to my house tomorrow," said Mrs. Lockwood. "He wants to take some photos of my greenhouse for his science project. Why don't you come over, too, Dee?"

"Great, I'll be there," Dee said. "Would it be all right if I brought a friend? I'm not sure yet if she wants to come."

Mrs. Lockwood turned up the gravel drive to the inn and stopped out front. "That would be fine," she replied.

Dee said a fast good-bye, then bounded up the steps and straight to her room. "I have the best news," she began as soon as Louisa materialized. She went on to tell Louisa all about the broken orchid and the bullies. " . . . And there he was—the answer to our problems actually lying there in the mud right at my feet!" she concluded.

"That's wonderful!" cried Louisa. "Of course I feel sorry for the poor boy, but I'm so glad you found him. I wonder if he has any brothers or sisters."

"Who knows, maybe he's got ten of them. We

only need one more anyway. Tomorrow we'll go over and see him," said Dee. "Our search has ended!"

"We?" Louisa questioned.

"I've been thinking about it," Dee explained. "Maybe all Jerry needs is someone to be nice to him. It might be real simple for you to help him just by doing that."

"Why do *I* have to be his friend?" Louisa objected.

"Because *you're* the one who has to help a relative. It won't do any good if I'm his friend. What's the problem?"

"I simply don't wish to be visible to anyone but you. You understand. It's awkward enough under normal circumstances. And now with . . . with . . . him, Matthew Duncan, out there . . . I'm frightened."

"No sweat, Louisa. We'll dress you in some of my clothing. Even if Matthew Duncan is around, he won't recognize you." Dee was beginning to feel very positive about things. They hadn't seen Matthew Duncan in a while. He was starting to seem like nothing but a bad dream to Dee. And now they'd found this third relative. Things were definitely looking up.

For the next hour Dee and Louisa sat and talked about what they might do for Jerry. Then

Dee went downstairs to help with supper. She met her father coming up. "How was school?" he asked.

"Great!" Dee told him brightly.

Mr. Forest looked surprised but pleased. "Glad to hear it. I'm just going up to take a shower before supper." Dee noticed that his hands were covered with soot. "I've been working on that old boiler all day," he explained. "Maybe now we can get some decent heat at night."

*Yes!* thought Dee. Things were most definitely looking up.

Down in the kitchen, Aunt Win was still in the middle of cooking. She told Dee she wouldn't be needing her for another hour or so.

Dee was about to go up to her bedroom when she spotted Eva sitting alone in the parlor writing something. "Hi," Dee said, coming up behind her.

Eva put her hand over her heart. "You scared me," she said, folding her paper quickly and putting it in the pocket of her long lavender cardigan.

"Sorry," said Dee. "Were you drawing?"

"No, just writing a letter." Dee sat down in the flowered armchair across from Eva. This was her chance to get to know her better. Dee was in such a good mood that she decided to give Eva another chance. Perhaps there was an explanation for all her actions.

"I've always wished I could draw," Dee said, "but I have no talent at all."

"Everyone has a little talent," Eva said. "You just have to—"

"Eva, draw a bird for me," Dee broke in. "Show me how to draw a bird, please? Any kind." Dee was suddenly seized with a desire to know, once and for all, if Eva was really who she said she was. She took a piece of white stationery from the rolltop desk across the room and placed it on the coffee table in front of Eva.

Eva's face flushed, and her delicate mouth turned down. "Okay, I will," she said, quickly regaining her composure. She took her pen and began drawing rapidly. "There," she said after only a minute.

Dee looked at the paper. It was a rather abstract drawing of trees and clouds with several squiggly lines to indicate birds. "What kind of birds are these?" Dee asked.

"They're birds in flight," Eva answered, getting up. "It's an easy way to depict birds if you're not really good at drawing. Since you said you couldn't draw, I thought it might come in handy for you."

"But—"

"You did say any kind of bird," Eva reminded her. "Excuse me, now. I have to wash up for supper." She flashed a wide smile and left Dee sitting alone in the parlor.

*I know when I've been had,* thought Dee. *Even I could draw birds like these.*

So Eva was a phony. This proved it. Didn't it? Dee thought it did, but she wanted to be sure.

Picking up the piece of paper, Dee hurried up to her room to get Louisa's opinion. As soon as the bedroom door closed, Louisa came into view. "I have something to tell you about Eva," Dee said excitedly.

"Who?" Louisa asked distractedly.

"Eva! You know, the woman who's staying at the inn who I think isn't telling us the truth about herself," said Dee all in one breath.

"Oh, yes," said Louisa. "What about Eva?"

Dee showed her the paper and asked if she thought it looked like the work of a real artist. "It isn't very detailed," Louisa agreed halfheartedly. Dee could see she wasn't interested in the subject. Her mind was clearly still on Matthew Duncan.

Louisa stood up slowly and glided over to the window. It was already dark and not even the full moon could fight its way through the thick cloud covering. With her back to Dee, Louisa stared out into the darkness—and then let out an earsplitting scream!

# CHAPTER
## 9

"Louisa! What is it!"

Dee ran over to the window and looked out. "Oh, my!" she gasped. Matthew Duncan, his black jacket flapping in the wind, stood at the base of the dogwood tree that was outside her window. He was barely visible, but the outlines of his sharp features were illuminated by the porch light. Dee could see that he was staring straight up at her bedroom window.

She jumped back and turned to Louisa, who was frantically clutching Dee's wrist. "Maybe he's just looking," Dee whispered, her heart pounding. "He might not really know you're here." Louisa and Dee leaned toward the window cautiously.

Matthew Duncan was beginning to climb the tree up to Dee's room!

They leapt back. Louisa covered her face with her trembling hands. "This is it. He's found me."

"Louisa, quick, disappear!" Dee urged her, and Louisa obeyed. Dee wasn't sure what to do next. She wanted to run downstairs, but she couldn't leave Louisa. They still hadn't decided whether Matthew Duncan could see her when she was invisible.

Desperately, Dee looked around the room. Her eyes fell upon the two *History of Misty Island* books. She grabbed both volumes from her desk and tucked them under her arm. Her hands shaking almost uncontrollably, she pushed up the window and hurled one, then the other heavy book at the man.

Then quickly, she slammed down the window and drew the curtains. Her heart was racing and her chest heaved with terror. She suddenly felt light-headed, as if she might faint. The ghost was still climbing the tree and was about to reach the bedroom window. He hadn't been a bad dream, after all.

Dee stood petrified with fear and indecision. There was nothing she could do to stop him. How could she keep him out? Even the walls

70

were no barrier to a ghost! She waited with her hands clenched into fists. Would he appear? Would the air stir as it did whenever Louisa materialized? Or would he come crashing through the window?

At that moment, the door burst open and her father came charging in. "Dee! That scream! Are you all right?"

Dee tried to look calm. "I stubbed my toe," she lied, checking the window quickly.

Her father followed her gaze. "What are you looking at?" he asked.

"Nothing. The tree. It banged against the window. It startled me."

Mr. Forest knelt down and began untying her sneaker. "Let me see that toe. Maybe it's broken." He looked up at her face. "Your foot. It's trembling. Dee, you're shaking all over. Are you in a lot of pain?"

Dee felt the tingle of tears just below her eyes. It was time, she decided, to tell her father everything. He would protect her.

"Dad," she began, "I—" But she couldn't go on. Louisa had made it clear that she didn't want anyone else to know of her existence. Besides, how could her father really help them? What defense did he have against a ghost, even if he did believe Dee's story? If Matthew Duncan came through that window now, they would all be helpless against him.

"What is it, Dee? What's the matter?" her father pressed.

"Yes, it hurts a lot. My toe, I mean," she said.

He took off her sneaker and sock and told her to wiggle her toes. "Nothing's broken," he concluded, "but I know a stubbed toe can hurt like crazy. Want me to bring you up some supper?"

Dee nodded.

"Here, let me help you into bed," her father said. "Keep your foot up and let me know if it starts to swell," he instructed before giving her a kiss and leaving the room.

Dee listened for his footsteps as he padded down the stairs. Then, taking a deep breath for courage, she got out of bed and crept across the room to the window. She had to know if the ghost was still there. Slowly, she pushed the curtain back a crack and peeked out.

Everything was still. He was gone. Disappeared.

Dee staggered back and held onto the bedpost, weak with relief.

Then she called softly to Louisa. "Where are you?"

"I'm here, on the bed." Louisa's voice sounded as if it were coming from far away.

"Well, come on. Make yourself visible."

"I'd rather not," Louisa said after a long pause. "I feel safer this way."

"But, Louisa, he's gone," Dee said, trying to control the anxiety in her own voice. "It's hard for me to talk to you when I can't see—"

"I don't care," Louisa interrupted. "Dee, Matthew Duncan knows where I am. He was on his way up to get me!" she said shrilly.

"But he *didn't* get you," Dee pointed out.

"What am I going to do?" Louisa asked hopelessly. "He won't run away next time. I'm surprised you were able to stop him this time. I just know he'll be back."

"Louisa, stop! You're letting yourself fall apart. I'll tell you the first thing we have to do. We have to go help your relative Jerry. Once we've done that, you'll have only one more relative to help, and then you'll be back with your family."

"I don't know, Dee," the trembling voice said from the direction of the closet. "I'm so afraid. I think I had better just stay in here."

"You have to come out with me, Louisa. You've got to force yourself."

"I suppose you're right," Louisa agreed faintly.

"I *am* right," said Dee. "Do you promise to come with me tomorrow?"

Silence.

"Come on, promise," Dee coaxed.

"All right. I promise," came Louisa's reluctant reply.

# CHAPTER

# 10

After school the next afternoon Dee hurried upstairs to drop off her books and pick up Louisa. The inn was deserted. Aunt Win had gone to visit a friend, and Dee didn't know where her father and Eva were.

"Louisa, are you here?" she called, tossing her backpack onto the bed.

"Yes, I'm here," came Louisa's voice.

"Louisa, please make yourself visible," Dee said, looking toward the bed. "You've got to get dressed if we're going to see Jerry."

Louisa slowly appeared, sitting on the edge of the bed. "I am dressed," she said. Her pale face seemed to shimmer and fade in the arc of light from the bedroom window. The auburn ringlets that surrounded her face gleamed like copper in the late afternoon sun.

Dee eyed her critically. "Your clothes are a hundred years old, Louisa. You can't let Jerry see you in those." Pulling a pair of jeans from her bottom dresser drawer, Dee tossed them on the bed. "Here, these are a little tight on me, so they should fit you perfectly. I'll find a top for you to wear with them."

"No, Dee . . . wait." Louisa held up the jeans and examined them, looking very troubled. "I can't wear trousers. I know you do, but it would feel too unnatural to me."

"You're wearing my sneakers."

"Shoes are one thing," said Louisa. "But pants are another!"

"You'll get used to them," said Dee impatiently. "Now come on. We have to get to Mrs. Lockwood's house."

Louisa stepped out of the pink high-top sneakers, put the pants on under her long dress, and stepped back into the shoes. Then she modestly disappeared in order to change into the blue sweatshirt Dee handed her. She rematerialized, looking extremely uncomfortable in her borrowed clothes.

"You look great," Dee told her.

"No, this won't work," Louisa said. "I don't see why I have to be visible."

76

"Because we want to do this quickly, remember. If all Jerry needs is a friend, then you have to be it. And he can't be friends with someone he can't see!"

Louisa thought about it, nervously chewing her lower lip. "All right. I'll be invisible until we get to the Lockwood house and then I'll appear. How would that be?"

"That sounds okay," said Dee. "You will appear, though?"

"I will. I promise."

Dee looked Louisa over. "That hair won't make it," she said, picking her brush up off the bureau top.

"Not my curls!" Louisa protested.

"Well, tie them back, at least," said Dee, holding out a rubber band. Louisa took it and pulled her hair into a ponytail.

"Okay, you look fine," said Dee. "Let's go."

The icy rain had finally stopped. It had washed away most of the snow, leaving behind a muddy landscape. Now a warm wind was blowing, warmer than anything Dee had felt all winter. "Maybe spring will come after all," she said as they walked toward Mrs. Lockwood's house. There was no answer. "Louisa, answer me," Dee demanded.

"Yes, I'm sorry," Louisa's voice replied. "I

was nodding in agreement. I forgot you couldn't see me."

Dee sighed. Louisa was really nervous. Matthew Duncan's appearance at the inn had obviously terrified her. Dee had to admit she'd found it pretty terrifying, too. But she couldn't let the fear stop her. She had to be strong for Louisa.

The girls rounded a curve in the narrow road and the Lockwood house came into view. It was a large, rambling place, set on a wide lawn behind a low picket fence.

Dee pushed open the gate and followed the walk up to the front door. Before she could reach for the door knocker, the door swung open. A startled Mrs. Lockwood stood in the doorway. She was wearing a brown tweed coat and a matching hat, obviously dressed for the outdoors.

"Dee!" Mrs. Lockwood cried. "You gave me a start. Why didn't you knock?"

"I was about to," Dee explained. "I came to see Jerry. Is he here yet?"

Mrs. Lockwood leaned close to Dee and lowered her voice confidentially. "No, he's not. And I'm a bit worried. My sister called and told me that yesterday he sneaked out of school at lunchtime and didn't come home until after supper. Apparently some boys had threatened to beat him up."

"You mean he was walking around in the rain all that time?" Dee asked sympathetically.

"Yes, he was," Mrs. Lockwood fretted.

"He's probably okay now," Dee consoled her. "Where are you going?"

"I have to take this letter to the post office before it closes. Otherwise I won't be eligible for the big May Day flower show. But I don't feel right leaving before Jerry gets here."

"Go ahead. We'll wait for him," said Dee.

Mrs. Lockwood's arched eyebrows shot up. "*We*, dear?"

Dee looked quickly over her shoulder and remembered that Louisa was still invisible. "I . . . um . . . I mean, my girlfriend might join me later. She's definitely going to join me. At least she *promised* she would," Dee said as much for Louisa's benefit as Mrs. Lockwood's.

"Well, good then. You'll be here when Jerry arrives. Tell him I'll return shortly." She pushed open the door and then headed down the walkway. When she was several feet away, Louisa came into view.

"Oh, Dee, I almost forgot—" Mrs. Lockwood turned on the path, and her hand flew up to her throat. "My heavens!" she cried at the sight of Louisa.

"Umm . . . this is the friend I was telling you about," said Dee, flustered.

"Where did *you* come from?" asked Mrs. Lockwood.

"She's very quiet," Dee said, laughing nervously. "Sometimes it seems like she pops in from nowhere."

"It certainly did," said Mrs. Lockwood, looking Louisa over. "You seem like a sweet girl, nonetheless. Jerry will be glad to see you both, I'm sure." Mrs. Lockwood headed back down the path, then stopped and turned around yet again. "I was going to tell you that if you like, you can go back to the greenhouse and look at my orchids. I have some beautiful cymbidiums."

"Thanks," said Dee, stepping into the house. "You'd better hurry, or the post office will close."

Louisa followed Dee into the front hall. From the doorway, they watched Mrs. Lockwood hurry to the garage to get her car.

"She's a nice lady," Louisa said as the black Plymouth slowly chugged off down the driveway.

"She is," Dee agreed. "Can you believe that you're her great-great-great-aunt or something like that?"

"I'd rather not think about it," said Louisa with a small shudder. "It's too strange."

Dee watched Louisa run her delicate fingers along the dark rolltop desk and over the back of a beautifully carved oak chair. "What is it?" she asked.

"This furniture once belonged to my aunt Rose," Louisa said. "I remember her saying she was giving it all away when she moved to Boston. It's strange to see it here."

Dee sensed a sadness, a longing for her old life, welling up in Louisa. "There are lots of memories on this island, aren't there?" she said kindly.

Louisa looked around the antique-filled room before answering. "It's as if one day everything was in place, and the next day it wasn't. Nothing makes sense anymore. Furniture I recognize is in the wrong home. The buildings I knew are gone. Or strange people live in the buildings that still stand. Some people, like Nicky Dodge, look like people I once knew, only they're *not* the people I knew. They're very distant relatives. Everything that once was mine is gone." A tear ran down Louisa's pale cheek.

Dee put her hand on her friend's shoulder. "Please don't be so sad," she said. "Things will be better soon. You may not be able to go back, but you can still go forward, and—"

She broke off at the sound of the front door opening and then slamming shut. Both girls hurried to the entranceway.

They stepped back in shock at the sight of Jerry Mason. His face and hands were muddy. His jacket was torn. His glasses were shattered. And a stream of blood trickled slowly down the side of his face.

# CHAPTER

# 11

"Jerry!" Dee cried. "Did those horrible boys from school do this?"

At first, Jerry was too startled to speak. He wiped his bleeding forehead with his dirty hand. "What are you doing here?" he asked, his voice shaky and high-pitched. "Where's my aunt?"

"She went to the post office," Dee told him. "Didn't Mrs. Lockwood tell you we were coming?"

Jerry took off his shattered glasses. The plastic frame split in half in his hand. "She told me, but I figured it was some kind of joke. It is a joke, isn't it?"

"We're not playing a joke, Jerry," said Dee. "This is my friend Louisa."

Jerry stared down at his broken glasses. "I'm not much in the mood for company," he said.

"Why do those boys want to beat you up all the time?" Dee asked.

"Why not?" Jerry muttered. He fingered the torn sleeve of his jacket. "They think it's funny."

"Is there anything we can do to help?" Dee asked, looking at Louisa, who still hadn't uttered a word.

"No. I'm going upstairs to get my aunt's camera. She said I could use it to take pictures of her greenhouse," he said glumly. He started up the stairs and then stopped. "If it's not a joke, then why did you two come to see me?"

"We just wanted to say hi," Dee replied. "Remember? We met yesterday in front of the school."

"Don't remind me." Jerry cringed. "What did you think I was doing? Admiring your boots?"

"Okay, it wasn't the best way to meet someone," Dee conceded. "But I don't know many people on the island and you seemed nice. My friend here wanted to meet some nice people, too. So, we thought we'd come over and see you."

Jerry looked skeptical. "I still think this is a joke," he said, "but I'll be right back, anyway." When he reappeared five minutes later, he had washed up and he had his aunt's instant camera. He laid it down on the hall table and joined Dee and Louisa, who had taken seats in the living room.

"Are you sure you girls aren't putting me on?" he asked.

"Putting you on what?" Louisa asked.

Dee quickly changed the subject. "What did you do to those boys to make them so mad at you?"

"Nothing," Jerry said. "They just pick on me—because I'm a little overweight, I guess."

"I would call you stocky, not overweight," said Louisa.

"Thanks," he answered, smiling for the first time since they'd met him. "There's always one kid in every class who gets picked on and it's always me."

"Maybe you just need a good friend," said Dee hopefully. "Don't you think that would solve your problems?"

"No," Jerry said firmly. "I need to make those guys stop picking on me. They know I'm not a fighter. That's why they keep doing it."

An uncomfortable silence set in. Louisa and Dee looked at Jerry and smiled. He smiled back.

"So . . ." said Dee.

"So . . ." Jerry replied.

"How do you spend your free moments?" Louisa asked, seeming genuinely interested.

"I watch TV mostly," he said. "I like old detective shows. I love all the old *Magnum, P.I.*s," he added, warming to the subject. "I also really like *Hawaii Five-O*. Stuff like that."

"Is a detective something like a police officer?" Louisa asked.

Jerry gave her a funny look. "This is where the joke starts, right?"

"There's no joke, Jerry," Dee assured him. "Louisa just doesn't watch a lot of television. Would you know what a detective was if you didn't watch TV?"

Jerry considered that for a moment. "I'm not sure. Maybe not. I've never actually met one. I don't even think there is a detective on Misty Island."

"You could be the first one," Louisa offered encouragingly.

Jerry's eyes lit up. "Wouldn't that be something! I would love that. I always try to solve little mysteries. I figured out who was stealing my mom's paper every day. I did a stakeout and everything. I sat in the bushes and waited all morning. Boy, was I stiff. But it was worth it. I was right there when that dog from across the street came by and grabbed the paper."

Louisa clapped her hands delightedly. "That was clever of you!"

"You think so?" asked Jerry, pleased. "I solved another case once. . . ."

Dee sat in silence as Jerry told Louisa his story. She wasn't really listening because she was hatching a plan. It would have been simple if Jerry simply needed a friend. But unfortunately what he needed was to get the bullies in school off his back. He needed some self-confidence. So far, the only time she'd seen him show any of that was just now, when he was talking about his detecting abilities.

"I'm sure glad we came by," Dee cut into Jerry's rather long story. "We have a mystery that needs solving, and you seem like the perfect person to help."

"Ha, ha, ha," said Jerry bitterly. "Now *this* is the joke. Sucker poor dumb Jerry into thinking he's solving a crime. Send him on some dumb wild-goose chase, and then tell all your friends about it."

"Boy, have you got a bad self-image," said Dee.

"Yes," Louisa chimed in, taking her cue from Dee. "It's a shame you don't believe us. We so need your help."

"Come on, Louisa," Dee said, getting up from

her chair. "I suppose we're wasting our time here."

Louisa followed Dee out to the front hall. "What mystery are we talking about?" she whispered.

"Shh," hissed Dee. "I'll tell you later."

"No—wait!" Jerry came running after them. "Do you really have a mystery to solve?"

"Yes, really," Dee said. "Do you want to help?"

"Absolutely," Jerry replied, actually grinning now. "I've watched enough detective shows. I think I'd be really good at it."

"We'd be very grateful," said Louisa.

"Meet us tomorrow after school at Misty Island Inn," Dee instructed. "We'll fill you in then."

Jerry looked disappointed. "Can't you tell me anything now?"

Dee looked from side to side, as if to make sure no one was eavesdropping. "All I can say is it involves tailing someone to see where she goes."

"I'm excellent at that," Jerry proudly assured them as they headed out the door.

"What mystery is Jerry going to solve?" Louisa asked as soon as they were outside.

"He's going to help us get the real story on Eva the so-called bird artist."

Louisa shivered. "I do hope this works," she said. "But I still don't see what's wrong with Eva Barlow. It's Matthew Duncan I'm worried about. I feel as if he's getting closer by the minute!"

# CHAPTER

# 12

The next morning, Dee woke up feeling hopeful. She sat up in bed and saw that once again it was raining. At least there was no more howling wind or sleet, she thought.

She rolled over in bed and thought about everything that had happened the day before. She'd found Jerry just in time. Louisa was right. Matthew Duncan was much too close for comfort. They no longer had the luxury of looking for Louisa's relatives at a leisurely pace. They had to get Louisa off Misty Island as fast as possible.

Dee only hoped that solving this mystery would help Jerry gain the confidence he needed. And while they were helping him, she thought, he just possibly might be helping them—or at least her.

Every day Dee could see that her father liked Eva more and more—whether he wanted to admit it to himself or not. If Eva wasn't who or what she claimed to be, there was a good chance her father would be hurt. Dee couldn't let that happen. He'd suffered enough already. And who knew? Maybe Jerry really was a good detective and he would discover the truth about Eva. In any case, Dee now had an excuse to follow the woman and see if she was really out sketching birds as she claimed.

Dee stretched and got out of bed, then slipped into jeans and a light blue sweater. Her father's tinkering with the boiler had yielded results. It was positively toasty in her room. She gave her hair a few swipes with a brush and went downstairs for breakfast.

Her good mood took a plunge when she saw her father's overnight bag standing by the front door. "Dad! What's going on?" she cried, hurrying into the kitchen.

Her father was seated at the kitchen table, a cup of coffee in his hand. Eva sat beside him, reading the morning paper. She smiled sleepily at Dee. "I'm just going away overnight," Mr. Forest said. "Some problem with a job in Brookline." He shook his head and grinned. "I guess they just can't get along without me. Don't look so worried, honey. I'll be back tomorrow morning. Promise."

Dee frowned and poured herself a bowl of cold cereal. She wanted to be mature about this, but he'd only just arrived. She didn't like the idea of his going away again. What if the job took longer than expected? Now that she'd gotten her father back, she wanted to keep him—especially with Matthew Duncan lurking around. For even though she was reluctant to tell him about the ghost, it made her feel a lot safer just knowing he was near.

"What are you going to do today?" Mr. Forest asked Eva casually. Dee's ears perked up as she waited for the woman's answer.

Eva yawned. "I don't know. I'm feeling kind of lazy. I might just spend the day reading." She raised her cup and finished her coffee.

Dee bit back a groan of disappointment. How were they going to tail Eva if she hung around and read all day? Watching Eva read was hardly the thing to boost Jerry's confidence!

After breakfast, Aunt Win offered Mr. Forest a ride to the ferry. She had to go into town anyway. She was spending the day volunteering at the hospital. Dee's father gave Dee a quick kiss on the forehead and dashed out behind Aunt Win. Minutes later Eva poured herself another cup of coffee and carried it back to her room.

"Louisa!" Dee called, finding herself alone in the kitchen.

Louisa slowly appeared in front of the oven. She was still wearing the same clothes she'd borrowed from Dee the other day. *Louisa is so pretty,* Dee thought. *Even in jeans and a sweatshirt she looks like a beautiful old-fashioned girl who's just stepped out of a photograph.* "Are you going to be all right?" Dee asked her.

"I think so," Louisa answered. "I was thinking about it last night. When we were both alive, I was brave enough to stand up to Matthew Duncan. Now I just have to find that same courage in myself again. That's all."

"That's the spirit!" said Dee. She suddenly blushed with embarrassment. "Oops, I did it again."

This time, though, Louisa laughed out loud. "That's all right. I'm going to try to be a spirit in good spirits if I can. It's better than being terrified all the time."

"Keep up the good work, and I'll come straight home from school," Dee said, grabbing her backpack. "And keep your fingers crossed that Eva doesn't hang out in her room all day."

Dee put on her boots and coat, then set off for school. Unfolding her umbrella, she headed down the drive. The rain was surprisingly warm.

Once again, Dee had trouble concentrating in class. Her mind was on the afternoon ahead. She looked for Jerry at lunchtime, but he was nowhere to be seen. At the end of the day there was still no sign of him. She was beginning to worry. She hoped he wasn't sick.

When Dee got back to the inn, everything was quiet. She was halfway up the stairs when the doorbell rang. She hurried down and opened the door. It was Jerry, and to her dismay, Dee saw that he was wearing a rumpled raincoat over a bright Hawaiian shirt and jeans. *Not exactly an outfit for tailing someone inconspicuously!* she thought.

She started to say something, but changed her mind. Her criticism certainly wouldn't build Jerry's confidence. "Would you like to come up to my room?" she asked him instead. "Louisa's there."

"Oh, okay," he said, peering nervously around the hall. Cautiously, he followed her up the stairs.

Louisa was already visible when they entered the room. "Hello, Jerry," she said pleasantly.

"That's a very colorful outfit you're wearing. I like it."

Dee looked at Louisa with puzzled eyes. Was she kidding—or just being kind? No, Louisa was always sincere. Apparently she did like the outfit. She never ceased to surprise Dee.

"Thank you," said Jerry. He stood there awkwardly until Dee told him to sit down in her desk chair. Then she quickly filled him in about Eva's suspicious behavior.

"The suspect sounds very suspicious indeed. I suggest we follow her," Jerry said seriously.

"Umm . . . yes," Dee agreed. "That was the plan. Here's what we're going to—" Dee broke off at the unmistakable sound of footsteps in the hallway. Tiptoeing quickly to the door, she opened it wide enough to poke her head out.

She could see Eva heading down the stairs. But even from behind, Dee could tell she was dressed for the outdoors in coat, boots, and scarf. "So much for Eva's lazy day of reading," Dee whispered.

Dee pulled her head back into the room. "Come on," she said to Jerry and Louisa. "Project Eva is about to begin."

# CHAPTER
# 13

"At least the rain has stopped," Jerry said as they followed Eva at what they hoped was a safe distance.

"Shh." Dee clamped her hand over his mouth. Possibly sensing their presence, Eva turned around suddenly. Dee, Jerry, and Louisa quickly ducked behind two tall pines.

They waited a few more minutes and then peeked around the trees. To their relief, Eva was continuing along the road with long, determined steps.

"Stay back," Dee whispered as they started off again. But that wasn't so easy to do. The road curved and curved again, and Eva had picked up her pace. Each time they lost sight of her, they'd hurry around the curve. Then they'd have to stop short and look for cover in case Eva decided to turn around again.

"Tailing people is harder than I thought," Jerry admitted.

They continued on past the boarded-up inns and shops. Louisa paused just before they came to the deserted guest house where they'd first seen Matthew Duncan. She looked at Dee nervously. Dee herself felt reluctant to walk past it.

"What's the problem?" asked Jerry, turning to see the two girls several yards behind him. "She's getting away from us."

"You're right, Jerry," said Dee. "Let's run for a bit." With their heads down, Dee and Louisa raced past the guest house as fast as they could. Jerry huffed and puffed his way behind them.

"Gee, you girls can run fast," he said, panting.

Ten minutes later they came to the edge of the quiet town. "We'll have to be careful that she doesn't spot us," Dee cautioned. "We can't exactly get lost in the crowd here."

Louisa looked down the empty, rain-soaked street. "I hate to be the bearer of bad tidings," she said, "but Eva has disappeared."

Jerry looked at Louisa with admiration. "I love the way you talk," he said.

"There she is—in front of Dodge's Fish Market," Dee cried, ducking behind the closed-up movie theater and beckoning the others to follow.

But Jerry just stood there, staring at Louisa. Her bright pink sneakers were planted smack in the middle of an ankle-deep puddle. "Didn't you notice that your feet are kind of wet?" he asked her.

Louisa had worn a raincoat and hat for appearance's sake. But she hadn't bothered with boots. "Oh, gracious, so I am." She giggled nervously.

"Come on," Dee said, scampering out of her hiding place and leading them down the street to the fish store. Peering through the big glass window, she saw Nicky helping his father place more ice in the long display counter. Before Dee could duck down, he saw her and flashed his broad smile.

Forgetting her mission for a moment, Dee smiled back. Then she felt Louisa's hand yank her back sharply. "We're on a case, remember," Louisa said.

"Right," Dee agreed, regaining her composure. "I thought Eva was here, but maybe she went into the coffee shop next door."

They peeked in the window there, too, but the shop was dimly lit. Squinting hard, Dee could make out Alice Kennicot, the owner, at her usual perch behind the cash register. There were two men hunched over coffee cups at the counter, but a wooden partition blocked Dee's view of the back booths.

"We'll have to go in," said Dee. "Jerry, you check behind the partition. Eva doesn't know you."

Jerry suddenly looked as pale as Louisa. "Me?" he gulped, his voice rising an octave. "I'm not sure I—"

"Come on." Pulling him by the sleeve of his wrinkled raincoat, Dee opened the door and stepped right in before Jerry could think of any excuses.

Jerry breathed in the tangy aroma of freshly made bacon as they walked to the back of the coffee shop. Keeping close to the partition, he peered slowly around the edge of it. Then he jumped back, almost knocking down Dee and Louisa, who stood right behind him. "She's there!" he said in a loud whisper.

"Shh!" said Dee and Louisa together. Slowly, the three of them took a look. There, seated across from each other and sipping coffee, were Eva and an older man with short, gray hair. The man wore a gray suit jacket over a pale blue Oxford shirt.

Dee and Louisa immediately stepped out of

view behind the partition. But Jerry seemed frozen to the spot. He stood there, staring at the back booth, until Dee pulled him back.

"What were you trying to do, read their lips?" Dee whispered.

But Jerry didn't answer her. He was already walking out the door. Louisa gave Dee a puzzled look, and then both girls hurried after him.

They caught up with Jerry on the sidewalk out front. "Jerry, what's wrong? What did you see back there?" Louisa asked.

"I noticed something when that guy reached for the sugar," Jerry explained in a shaky voice. "He's wearing a shoulder holster under his jacket."

"Do you mean he has a gun?" Louisa gasped.

Jerry nodded. "That's exactly what I mean."

Dee stared at him skeptically. "Are you sure?"

"Believe me," Jerry told her. "I've watched enough cop shows to know when someone is armed. And this guy definitely is."

"Good work, Jerry," Louisa said. "You truly are a fine detective."

Jerry blushed. "Not really."

"What could Eva be doing with that guy?" Dee wondered aloud. And, turning to Jerry, "What do you think they're up to?"

But once again Jerry didn't answer. He was

staring past the girls with a look of disappointment on his face.

"Oh, no!" he cried. Dee and Louisa followed his gaze and saw a blue hatchback turning the corner. "It's my mother," Jerry exclaimed. "She must be looking for me. I forgot to tell her where I was going. See you guys later." With a quick wave, he ran to the car and got in.

"What do we do now?" asked Louisa.

"I guess we go home," said Dee.

They had taken just a few steps down the street when Eva and her companion came out. Dee dived into the alley between the coffee shop and the fish market. Checking from side to side, she realized that Louisa had disappeared. She wished she could become invisible, too. If Eva so much as glanced to the left, she was sure to see Dee pressed to the wall.

But Eva was looking right at her companion. "I don't want any innocent people getting hurt," Dee heard her say uneasily.

"I know, I know," the man replied.

"I hear The Seagull Inn is kind of a dump," Eva said in a more conversational tone. "How are you doing over there?"

"You heard right," the man replied. "Sounds like you got the better inn."

"My place really is nice. Too bad you can't

stay there, too, but we shouldn't be seen to-gether. Even this is too dangerous." The man nodded his head in agreement, then walked off quickly without even saying good-bye.

Dee didn't move for a long time. "Louisa, did you hear that?" she asked finally.

"Yes, I did." Louisa's voice was right beside her. "What do you think it means?"

"I don't know, but I think we'd better find out—and fast."

# CHAPTER

# 14

Just as Dee had feared, that night her father called from the mainland to say he would be delayed several more days on the Brookline job. "You sound upset," he told her over the crackling line of their bad connection.

"I'm okay," Dee answered.

"Good. Well, give Aunt Win a hug for me . . . Oh, and tell Eva that I picked up a copy of that book I was telling her about."

"What book is that?" Dee asked.

"Just a little book of poems," he answered casually. "She'd never read Yeats and I thought she'd like him."

Dee sighed. This was getting serious. Now he was buying Eva poetry books!

"Are you sure you're okay?" her father asked again.

"Yes, but there's something I think I should tell you," Dee began, but at that moment the line crackled with static once again. "Are you still there, Dad?" she asked when it cleared.

"Yes. I can barely hear you, though," he shouted over the line. "I have to get back to the job now, anyway. I'll call back later."

"Okay, Dad, but just let me—"

"I can't hear you, honey." His voice cut her off. "Talk to you soon."

"Bye," Dee said, slowly hanging up the phone. She had to tell him about Eva. There he was wandering around the bookshops of Brookline, picking out poems for her, while Eva was off having secret meetings with some guy with a gun!

A small sound made Dee whirl around. And there was Eva, standing in the doorway. It suddenly seemed to Dee that Eva moved with the silence of a cat, always popping up unexpectedly. "Everything all right?" the woman asked. "You look worried."

"Everything is fine," Dee said icily, and hurried up the stairs.

\* \* \*

Over the next few days the weather became warmer and drier. Every day after school, Jerry showed up at the inn and they resumed their project of tailing Eva. Although the rain had finally stopped and the mud was now caked and dry, Jerry continued to wear his Hawaiian shirt and old raincoat. It was obviously his idea of appropriate detective wear.

In the course of their investigation, they came to one conclusion. Eva was clearly searching for someone or something. She went to unlikely places like the old boatyard and the abandoned mill at the lake. Alone or with the man with the gun, she crisscrossed the island's many back roads. Once they even followed her to the high bluffs on the deserted south shore.

"This is hard work," Jerry muttered as they clambered down the steep, rocky slope of the bluff. They'd followed Eva along the deserted beach, ducking behind boulders to avoid being seen. But neither they nor Eva found anything remarkable there.

Later that same day Eva came to a small hut in the woods near Fingers Cove. She spent a long time inside, rummaging through the dirty shelves. When she finally came out, the distracted look in her eyes told them she hadn't found what she was looking for.

"For someone who doesn't know this island, she sure does get around," Dee noted as they scrambled back up the bluff behind Eva.

"I've lived on this island all my life and Eva has found places I never knew existed," said Louisa, climbing easily behind Dee.

Jerry looked at Louisa quizzically. "I've lived on this island all my life, too. How come I've never seen you?"

Louisa looked to Dee, but Dee was stumped. "I have private tutors," she said. "I've been ill."

"You have?" said Jerry sadly. In the few days they'd spent together, he'd grown increasingly fond of Louisa.

"I'm better now," she assured him. "Don't worry."

"Here, let me help you up the hill," Jerry offered, reaching his hand out to Louisa. Dee shot Louisa a warning glance. If Jerry felt the strange lack of heat or cold in Louisa's hand, he might suspect something.

But Louisa was already extending her hand, and Jerry registered nothing unusual as he helped her climb the last few yards up the hill. "Thank you, Jerry," Louisa said when they got to the top. "You're a very kind boy. If people knew you better, they would see that."

106

Jerry looked away. "I don't want to be kind. I want to be tough."

"Oh, no. It's much better to be kind, believe me," said Louisa.

Dee listened to them talk, a somewhat puzzled look on her face. It was clear that Louisa and Jerry had found some gentle connection. Though Dee often grew impatient with Jerry's awkward ways, Louisa seemed to admire him. Her sweetness touched Jerry and brought him out of his shell. Dee resolved to follow her friend's example and try to be less sharp with people in the future.

By the end of the week, the three sleuths knew every step Eva had taken, at least from the time school let out. Every day she went someplace different and every evening she and the man with the gun met in the coffee shop. And not once did she stop to sketch a bird of any description!

A warm, wet breeze blew over the island on Saturday morning. Dee could smell the ocean in it. A robin perched on her windowsill, the first Dee had seen all season. She took a deep breath and stretched lazily in bed.

Louisa appeared in Dee's room holding a small

yellow wildflower she'd picked. "It's definitely spring again," she said softly. "I am grateful to see another one." Her blue eyes were soft with memory and longing. "Oh, Dee, I can't tell you how much you appreciate everything when you realize that at any minute it might be gone. I don't know what's on the other side. I suppose it's very beautiful. But the earth is what I know." She nuzzled the fragrant petals.

Dee didn't like this talk of other worlds. It was all too confusing for her to comprehend. Louisa was her friend. That was all she really wanted to think about.

"I wish we could figure out this thing with Eva," Dee grumbled. "My father's coming back today and I don't know what to tell him."

"*I* wish we could find a way to make Jerry feel more confident," said Louisa. "The whole purpose of this detective business was to help him so that I can be closer to leaving before Matthew Duncan finds me."

"We haven't seen him in a while," Dee said hopefully.

"Oh, he's still here," Louisa said. "I can feel it in my bones. It's as if I can even hear him breathing, getting closer all the time. I wish I knew what he was waiting for. Why doesn't he just come and get me and be done with it?" she cried.

"Louisa, stop it!" said Dee. "You're letting this get to you. Stay calm. We're going to help Jerry and then you'll only need to help one more relative. You'll be safe soon."

"Anybody home?" came a deep voice from the front hall.

"It's Dad!" Dee said to Louisa. "I have to go down. Are you okay now?"

Louisa nodded.

"I'll be right back," said Dee. She ran downstairs and greeted her father with a hug.

After filling her in on his week, he said, "Guess what was on the ferry coming over with me? . . . A carnival! The boat was jammed with rides and carnival workers. They're setting up in the parking lot at the dock."

"Mercy, is it that time already?" said Aunt Win, drying her hands on her apron as she walked in from the kitchen. "That carnival comes here every year. It's as much a sign of spring as the geese returning."

"I was up half the night working so I could be back for the weekend," Mr. Forest said wearily, running a hand through his hair. "But I haven't been to a carnival since I was a kid. You want to go, don't you?"

"Sure, Dad, but first I want to tell you—"

"Can it wait?" he asked, yawning. "I want to

take a quick shower and a long nap, and then tonight we'll check out that carnival."

"Sure, it can wait," Dee said with a sigh.

Jerry arrived a few minutes later, but only to say that his parents wanted him to stay around the house and do some chores. "They're getting suspicious because I'm hardly ever home anymore and I never tell them where I've been," he explained. "I think they want me where they can see me."

As Dee watched him walk away, she thought she detected a slight spring in his step that hadn't been there before. Their adventures of the last few days had at least lifted his spirits.

Dee went upstairs and told Louisa about the carnival. "That sounds like fun," Louisa said wistfully.

"It does, doesn't it?" Dee said. "Why don't you come, too?"

"I don't think that's a good idea," Louisa protested. "It would be too dangerous."

Dee sat on the bed. "Speaking of danger," she said, "I wouldn't feel right leaving you here alone . . . just in case . . . well, you know."

"In case Matthew Duncan comes back," Louisa finished for her.

# CHAPTER

# 15

That night, Dee climbed into the front of the Jeep with Aunt Win. Mr. Forest had invited Eva to join them. Dee could barely take her eyes off the woman who sat beside her father, looking sweet and innocent in her pretty pink sweater and jeans. What was she up to?

The carnival was strictly small-town stuff, with only seven or eight rides and two rows of try-your-luck game booths. Even so, its arrival was clearly a highlight of the season, as Aunt Win had said. From the size of the crowd, it seemed that nearly everyone on the island had shown up.

A hot-dog cart, cotton-candy wagon, and popcorn stand occupied one end of the parking lot. On the other end stood a Haunted House with its labyrinth of distorted mirrors.

A small Ferris wheel had been set up just inside the lot. There were several kiddie rides, already filled with laughing, screaming children. Beyond them were more grown-up rides with names like Twister and Sonic Tornado.

Aunt Win caught sight of old Jack Dodge and went over to him, leaving Dee alone with her father and Eva. Louisa stood invisibly at her side. "Maybe we should start slow," said Dee, thinking of Louisa.

Her father gave her a startled look. "That's not like you, Dee. You usually can't wait to try the rides where you're twirling on your head or hanging by your fingernails."

Eva laughed. "Maybe your daughter's getting sensible in her old age," she joked, smiling at Dee.

Dee had to fight back her own smile. It had been easy to think of Eva as a criminal, a spy, or something equally sinister while they were tracking her from a distance. But it wasn't as easy up close. Eva seemed so *nice*. Dee reminded herself not to be fooled by appearances.

"Let's go on the Ferris wheel," Eva suggested, breaking the uncomfortable silence that had fallen between them.

"That's so high up," Louisa whispered in Dee's ear.

Dee nodded. "Would you mind if I went on the Ferris wheel by myself?" Dee asked her father and Eva.

"I wouldn't mind," Mr. Forest said, "but why would you want to do that?"

"Scarier that way," said Dee.

"Are you sure?" he asked doubtfully. "I thought you wanted to go slow."

"Not that slow. It's much better alone," Dee insisted.

"Well, okay." He handed her the strip of tickets he'd bought when they arrived. "I guess we'll be over by the game booths."

"Thanks," said Dee, heading for the Ferris wheel. She hoped her father would be all right alone with Eva. She glanced at the large canvas bag Eva had slung over her shoulder and wondered if she was carrying a gun, too.

Dee shrugged off her worry. What could Eva do to him here, in the middle of all these people? "Come on," she urged Louisa, holding up the strip of tickets. "I have a feeling you're going to love this." She led Louisa to the Ferris wheel, assuring her in low whispers that it was a perfectly safe and calm ride.

When she got to the front of the line, Dee

handed the operator two tickets. He stopped chewing his big wad of gum and stared at her strangely. "Watcha got there—an invisible friend?" Then he laughed hard at his own joke.

Flustered, Dee took back the extra ticket and climbed into the waiting Ferris wheel seat. "Sit in the middle," the operator instructed her.

"I like the side," she told him sharply.

He shrugged and pulled the lever that started the wheel moving. "Oh!" Louisa let out a small gasp as their seat lifted up into the air. "It's so lovely. What a splendid feeling!" Dee could almost picture the look of rapture on her friend's face, and it made her smile.

The wheel stopped with a jolt as other passengers were let on down on the ground. Seconds later, it began to spin again.

"I've never been up this high in my life," Louisa said happily as their seat swayed gently in the starry sky.

"Do you think you could float up this far?" Dee asked as they reached the top of the wheel.

"I don't know. I'd be scared to try," Louisa answered. "Oh, look at the people so far below. And all the lights! Have *you* ever been this high up before?"

"Higher," said Dee. "I was in an airplane once."

"Oh, my soul," came Louisa's awed voice. "The church steeple was the highest point on Misty Island. I think it still is. One time Tobias Dodge and I climbed up and looked down. It was exciting, but not like this."

They dipped until they'd gone full circle, then started to climb again. "This must be what it feels like to fly up to heaven," Louisa said dreamily.

The words caught Dee by surprise. Before she realized it, she had tears in her eyes. Poor Louisa, so far from heaven, so far from her family.

They spun in silence for a while longer, and a few minutes later their chair swung to a stop on the ground. The operator lifted the safety bar and they stepped down.

Dee was still feeling a little giddy from the ride as she walked away from the wheel. Her eyes searching the crowd for a glimpse of her father, she bumped right into a man who was standing directly in her path.

"I'm sorry—" she began, looking up apologetically. "I—" But Dee never finished her sentence. Her jaw dropped open when she saw who it was . . .

The ghost of Matthew Duncan!

# CHAPTER

# 16

"**Y**ou!" Dee blurted out. She wanted to back away but stood frozen with fear. She felt Louisa's nails digging into her arm.

The ghostly green eyes narrowed, then slowly widened again in recognition. Except for his eyes, Matthew Duncan's face remained expressionless, as blank and white as paper.

As Dee finally took a step back, she noticed that he was wearing the same black jacket, buttoned to the top even though it was a very warm night. He stared at her, as if trying to decide what to do.

"Sorry I bumped into you," Dee finally managed to say. She took a deep breath and brushed quickly past him on shaky legs.

"Hey!" he called after her. His voice was deep and raspy, as though it hadn't been used in a long, long time.

Dee kept going, picking up her pace, not looking back, trying to lose herself in the crowd.

"Hey—"

Now Dee began to jog. Glancing back over her shoulder, she saw Matthew Duncan close on her heels.

"He can see me!" Louisa moaned in Dee's ear. "I know he can!"

"Hurry. This way," Dee said, too frightened to think clearly. She broke through the line for the Twist-a-whirl. Glancing back again, she saw that he was gaining on them. If only she could find her father. The carnival grounds weren't that big. Where could he and Eva be?

Dee was running at full speed now, trusting that Louisa could keep up. She bumped into a little girl, knocking her to the ground. The girl started to cry as Dee helped her up.

Sensing Matthew Duncan closing in on her, she took off again. She tore through the line to one of the kiddie rides, turned sharply, and dashed behind a row of game booths. And still she felt Matthew Duncan steadily on her.

"Hey, you!" His rasping, ghostly voice sent a chill down Dee's back. She turned and saw him roughly push a teenage boy out of the way in his attempt to catch up to her.

"In here!" Dee cried to Louisa, heading up the steep ramp to the Haunted House.

"No!" Louisa called. "Please!"

The ticket-taker saw Dee hesitate at the door. "Step right in, honey," he said with a grin. "You're not afraid of ghosts, are you?"

"Come on, hurry," Dee pleaded to Louisa.

"I'm going as fast as I can," the ticket-taker said. Dee pushed two tickets into his hand and raced into the pitch-black darkness of the Haunted House.

Just inside, a hidden fan blew a blast of hot air into Dee's face. She took a few blind steps forward, waiting for her eyes to adjust. The passageway was so narrow, there was only enough room for one person to squeeze through at a time. Eerie red lights flickered on the black walls. Fiendish laughter rattled endlessly from a speaker somewhere above her.

"Louisa, are you here?" she called.

Some kids shrieked in mock terror from another passageway. Another stream of hot air blasted across Dee's face. A plastic skull popped out from the wall.

"Yes, I am," came Louisa's reply. "Why have we entered this dreadful place?"

"To lose Matthew Duncan," Dee told her. "He'll never find us here." Dee followed the curve of the passageway, which led to a small chamber dimly lit by a single purple bulb. Streamers of gauze hanging from the ceiling brushed against her face. But Dee hardly noticed the spooky effects. Compared with Matthew Duncan, they weren't the least bit frightening.

"He's going to find us," Louisa said, a note of panic in her voice. "He'll come right through the walls."

"Follow me," Dee said, slapping the gauze away from her face. "We'll just stay in here for a while until we're sure he's lost us. Then we—"

She broke off in amazement as a tall, thin figure burst into the purple room. Squinting in the darkness, Dee saw immediately that it was Matthew Duncan. How had he found them so easily? Maybe he really could pass right through walls!

"This way," Dee whispered, moving quickly along the passage. The dim light faded completely after the first turn, and the narrow passageway divided into three corridors. Dee hurried into the one on the left.

"He's coming for me," Louisa cried, right behind her. "I knew there was no hiding from him."

"Just keep going!" Dee urged desperately.

Moving blindly through the narrow passageway, Dee was sure she could feel Matthew Duncan's eerie presence behind her. Then suddenly, she felt that she and Louisa were alone again. "Hey!" She heard him shout from the middle corridor. He had taken a wrong turn.

"Quick! Maybe we can lose him now," Dee whispered. She made a sharp right through a curtain of black beads, icy cold to the touch, and entered a huge, barren room.

"Oh!" Dee cried out, nearly bumping into herself.

It was a chamber of mirrors, a maze of dark reflections and twisting passages. "Ouch!" She bumped her head, mistaking a mirror for an opening in the wall.

"Are you all right?" Louisa asked anxiously.

"Yeah. Fine. Let's get out of here," Dee whispered. And holding her hands in front of her as a shield, she tried to make her way through the labyrinth of mirrors.

"No!" Louisa saw him first. Matthew Duncan's face was reflected in six mirrors. Was he right behind them, by their side, or in some distant corner of the mirrored room? It was impossible to tell. He seemed to be everywhere at once, surrounding them, cutting off any chance for escape.

"Stay calm," Dee whispered, more to herself than Louisa. "It's only his reflection. He can't be in six places at once—can he?"

She took a step forward and hit another mirror.

Her head spinning, Dee looked up just in time to see Matthew Duncan make a grab for her with both of his arms. She screamed and reached out to fight him off.

But his big pale hands grabbed nothing but air. He was seeing her reflection at the same time she was seeing his.

"This way," Dee whispered. But there didn't appear to be a way out. She was about to panic completely when her hand suddenly went through an opening to the right. She stepped quickly into another corridor of mirrors, and again a half-dozen menacing Matthew Duncans were reflected all around her.

Now it was Louisa who panicked. "He's got us! We're trapped!" she cried.

"No! Keep moving! This way!" Dee told her.

Matthew Duncan lunged at them again. This time his head hit the glass with a loud *thunk*. He cursed and cried out in pain. Then, moving quickly, he stomped through a passageway and disappeared from Dee's view.

"Great!" Dee whispered. "He's gone the wrong way."

"He'll just turn around and find us," Louisa whispered hopelessly. "We've got to get out of here."

"I'm trying," Dee told her. She turned a corner, and then another, feeling carefully along the mirrored wall, trying not to collide with glass.

"Oh!" Matthew Duncan peered at her from directly ahead. Was that his face in a mirror—or was he standing right in front of her?

Dee turned and tried to go back, but she hit a mirror. She turned again. And again she saw his face looming larger, closer. A smile slowly formed on his pale lips.

Dee backed away. She still couldn't tell if he was ahead of her or behind her. But one thing she knew for sure—he was definitely moving closer!

She pressed her back against the glass, searching frantically for an escape route. But she couldn't find one.

Dee raised her hands protectively as the six Matthew Duncans, smiling broadly now, moved in to grab her.

# CHAPTER

# 17

Suddenly the floor started to creak and then revolve. Dee nearly stumbled. She steadied herself by pushing her arms against the mirror in front of her. But the mirror was spinning, too. Everything was spinning, including her.

Matthew Duncan's startled face slid slowly off the mirrors. Dee watched him make one last desperate grab for her before he disappeared entirely from view.

Only then did Dee realize she was standing on some sort of revolving floor, like a turntable. It spun around and clicked into place. She blinked once, twice—and then found herself standing outside. By sheer luck she had stumbled upon the exit from the

Haunted House. And Matthew Duncan was still inside.

"Come on, Louisa!" she cried, leaping down off the platform and onto the ground. "Are you here?"

"Y-yes," Louisa replied uncertainly.

Dee ran as fast as she could across the grass, heading back into the crowd. She hadn't gone far when she bumped into her father and Eva at the dart-tossing booth.

"There you are," Mr. Forest said, smiling. "Eva and I have been looking all over for you."

Eva tossed a dart and cried out happily when it burst a red balloon. "What do I win?" she asked the tired-looking girl behind the counter.

"Want to play some darts?" Mr. Forest asked Dee, reaching for his wallet. When she remained silent, he finally noticed the distressed look on her face. "Honey, what's wrong?"

"Nothing," Dee said, looking anxiously over her shoulder. "There was a man—"

Her father's face tightened with immediate concern. "What? What man?"

Dee decided she'd better not get into it. There was no way she could explain to her father that a man who might be a ghost was chasing after her and her friend, who truly was a ghost, for a reason neither of them knew for certain.

"No. No man. It was nothing," she corrected herself, forcing her mouth into a smile. "I'm just tired, Dad. Could we go home now?" she asked desperately just as a jacketed man emerged from the Haunted House.

"Oh, Dee," her father began. "It's still early. Eva and I—"

But Dee couldn't wait for him to finish his sentence. She knew Matthew Duncan would soon pick up her trail again. "Never mind, Dad," she interrupted. "I can walk home. It isn't far," she shouted as she began running across the carnival ground.

Dee hurried out of town and up the winding road that led to the inn. At the top of the hill she stopped, gasping for breath. "Are you okay?" she asked Louisa. "Let me see you."

Dee waited in silence for a few seconds as Louisa slowly came into view. They stood there together, looking back toward town, watching the white lights of the Ferris wheel revolve.

Then Louisa turned to Dee and shuddered. "We must get home. He'll be coming after us."

Dee's eyes widened as Louisa paled alarmingly in the moonlight. In one terrible moment she became so pale Dee could see right through her. Then the ghost girl began to flicker, wavering between visibility and invisibility before fading totally from view.

"Louisa, are you still here?" Dee cried, suddenly afraid that she'd lost her friend forever.

"I'm here," Louisa replied softly, right by her side.

Somewhat reassured, Dee began walking again. But she kept looking back over her shoulder, half expecting to see the frightening figure in black closing in.

# CHAPTER
# 18

"Come *on*, Louisa! Jerry will be here any minute," said Dee.

"I don't care," Louisa said from somewhere near the bed. "I don't want to see anyone. And I certainly don't want anyone to see me."

It was early the next afternoon and Louisa, still terrified by her narrow escape from Matthew Duncan, was refusing to materialize.

"But you *have* to see Jerry," Dee pleaded, sitting at the dressing table and pulling a hairbrush through her hair. "How else are you going to help him?"

"It doesn't matter anymore," Louisa muttered glumly. "I don't see the point of it."

"You can't hide here forever," Dee scolded.

Louisa didn't reply. "Jerry's coming over to help us search Eva's room and look for clues. He's so excited about this. He thinks he's a real detective. I'm sure we can help him, Louisa. But not if you just sit here waiting for Matthew Duncan to show up." Still no reply from Louisa, who was being unusually stubborn.

The chase through the Haunted House must have really terrified her, Dee realized. She shivered involuntarily at the memory of the dark, narrow passages, the horrifying chamber of mirrors, Matthew Duncan's reflection surrounding them everywhere they ran, their desperate escape.

"Dee—Jerry's here!" Aunt Win shouted from downstairs.

"Tell him to come up!" Dee shouted back. She got up from the dressing table and walked over to where she thought Louisa was sitting on the bed. "Hurry, Louisa. Make yourself visible. Jerry will be here in two seconds."

She could hear Jerry's heavy footsteps slowly climbing the creaky wooden stairs. "Come on, Louisa," Dee pleaded. "He really needs you!"

Louisa slowly came into view, looking paler than ever and very frightened. Dee reached over, took her hands, and pulled her off the bed. "Now, just put a smile on your face. Come on. You can do it."

Louisa's mouth quivered but couldn't quite manage a smile.

Jerry walked in, out of breath from his climb. "Hi, you two," he said, plopping down on the bed.

"Hi, Jerry. Did you go to the carnival last night?" Dee asked.

He shook his head. "Nope. My mom wasn't feeling well, so we—" He stopped to stare at Louisa. "Wow! What are you dressed up for?"

"Oh. I . . . well . . ." Louisa looked helplessly to Dee.

Dee hadn't even noticed that Louisa was wearing her own nineteenth-century clothes—the high-necked white blouse and the pleated black jumper that came down to her ankles.

"It's a great outfit, isn't it?" Dee chimed in. "We found it in an old trunk in the basement. Louisa tried it on just for fun."

"It's weird-looking," Jerry said, "but I like it. It looks as if it came from a history book or something."

"Yes. It really is weird-looking," Louisa agreed, forcing a laugh.

"Why don't you go into the closet and change back into your real clothes," Dee told Louisa. Louisa gratefully followed Dee's advice, emerging a few minutes later in a pair of Dee's faded jeans and a bright turquoise top.

They waited until they heard Eva's and Mr. Forest's footsteps going past Dee's door and down the stairs. Then they waited for the front door to slam.

"Okay. Back to Project Eva," Jerry said as soon as it did. He rubbed his hands together with exaggerated eagerness.

"We'll have to be careful not to move anything in Eva's room," Dee warned. "We don't want her to know we were snooping around in there."

"Of course not," Jerry said. "Good detectives don't leave a trace." He stepped out into the hallway and looked up and down the long corridor.

"I still don't think this is right," Louisa said, hanging back.

"Don't be silly, Louisa," Dee said. "We're not doing any harm. We're just going to look for clues to Eva's real identity."

"But we're trespassing, Dee, and—"

Dee gave her an impatient look. "Sshh. Let's go," she whispered.

They crept silently down the hall even though the second floor was now deserted and there was no one to hear them. "What about your aunt?" Louisa whispered, trailing behind.

"Aunt Win is in the cellar making blueberry preserves," Dee told her. "She'll be down there most of the day."

"Good," said Jerry.

"Listen, when we get there, Jerry, you check the closet," Dee instructed. "Louisa, you do her dresser. I'll take the rest of the room."

Jerry put a warning finger to his lips as they continued slowly down the hall.

*"Dee!"*

Dee's heart skipped a beat, and Jerry cried out in alarm.

"Dee! Are you up there?" It was only Aunt Win, calling from the foot of the stairs.

"What is it, Aunt Win?" Dee called down.

"I'm going out for a while," Winnifred shouted. "Anything you need in town?"

"No, I don't think so," Dee said.

"All right. I won't be long."

Dee relaxed a bit as the front door banged shut behind her aunt. But even though they were now completely alone, Louisa and Jerry still crept along the corridor as if expecting someone to jump out and catch them in the act.

When they came to Eva's door, Jerry cautiously turned the knob and pushed on the door, but it wouldn't budge. He turned the knob again and pushed harder. Still the door wouldn't move.

"She locked it," Dee said, not really surprised.

"I guess she doesn't trust us," Jerry said. "Or else she has something to hide."

"That's right," said Dee. "We have to get in there. Any ideas?" she asked, turning to look at Jerry. But he was staring at the side of Louisa's head.

"What is it?" asked Louisa, pushing her hair back self-consciously.

"Is that a hairpin you have there?" he asked.

"Yes. It holds the hair out of my face," she said. "Why do you ask?"

"Can I have a look at it?" Jerry asked. Louisa pulled the pin from her hair and handed it to him. "Wow! This is a real old-fashioned one."

"It was my grandmother's," Louisa fibbed. "What are you going to do with it?"

"People on TV are always picking locks with hairpins," he explained, looking quite pleased at the prospect.

"Do you know how to do it?" Dee asked doubtfully.

"I once read an article on lock picking in a detective magazine," said Jerry. He knelt down and set to work fiddling in the lock with the hairpin. Dee and Louisa stood by nervously.

"How's it going?" Dee asked after a minute.

"It feels like there's a little metal thing in here. If I could just push it—"

"Shhh!" Dee cut him off. She'd heard a sound coming from upstairs. The third floor was supposedly empty. "Did you hear that noise?" she asked Jerry and Louisa.

They had!

"What do you think it is?" Jerry asked.

All three of them looked up to the ceiling. The sound had definitely come from upstairs.

"Squirrel got in, maybe," Dee said hopefully.

"It doesn't sound at all like a squirrel," Louisa said, suddenly looking very frightened.

They heard it again, louder this time. "It sounds like scraping," Jerry said, listening hard. "Someone is scraping something."

The scraping stopped. They listened, eyes glued to the ceiling even though there was nothing to see.

"Maybe it was just the wind," Jerry suggested.

"I never heard wind like that," Dee said.

The scraping sound started again, then stopped. A minute later it was replaced by a light tapping.

"Is anyone staying upstairs?" Jerry asked, getting to his feet.

"No," Dee said softly. "No one. Eva's the only guest at the inn."

"Maybe it's a workman," Louisa suggested, brightening a little.

"Yeah. A construction worker." Jerry liked the idea, too. "Maybe your aunt is having new windows put in, or a crack in the wall fixed, or something like that."

Dee shook her head. "No. I'm pretty sure she would have told me."

The noise upstairs continued, even louder now.

"We'd better go investigate," Dee said.

Reluctantly, they tiptoed down the hall and up the creaking stairs. The third floor looked exactly like the second. As they inched their way along the narrow hallway, the scraping kept getting louder.

Outside room 3B, Dee motioned her friends to stop. The sound was definitely coming from there.

Dee took a deep breath and pushed open the door. She stepped into the room, Louisa and Jerry just behind her.

A man in gray overalls was bent over the radiator against the wall, his back to them, working feverishly with a chisel and hammer.

"Oh, good," Dee said. "It *is* a workman. Aunt Win must have forgotten to tell me."

134

But at the sound of her voice, the worker turned around and jumped quickly to his feet. Dee almost fainted with fright when she saw his pale, pale face. It wasn't a workman after all.

It was Matthew Duncan!

# CHAPTER
# 19

Dee tried to back out of the room. But she bumped into Jerry, who stumbled backward, and the two of them toppled to the floor.

"Sorry!" Jerry cried, getting slowly and awkwardly to his feet.

It was too late now to flee. Matthew Duncan had run to the door and pulled it shut. He stood in front of it, barring their way.

Dee looked at Louisa, who seemed paralyzed with fright. Her eyes were wide, her hands frozen at her sides. And her shoulders were slumped with resignation, as if she were ready to accept her fate—to go off to some cold, dark place with this cold, dark spirit.

But Dee wasn't about to let him take Louisa

without a fight. "Who are you? What are you doing here?" she cried, anger beginning to replace her fear.

Matthew Duncan ignored the question. He glared at Dee and pointed an accusing finger at her. "You've been trying to get in my way ever since I arrived," he said, his voice frighteningly calm. "Everywhere I go, there you are."

"Now, wait," Dee said. "I haven't been following you, if that's what you think."

"Oh, no?" he challenged her. "Then how come I can't make a move without bumping into you?"

Dee didn't know how to answer. Was he crazy? She and Louisa hadn't been following him. He'd been following them!

"Never mind," he said, frowning. "It doesn't matter anymore." He stared at Dee for a long silent moment and then lunged forward with surprising speed and grabbed her by the shoulders.

Dee tried to escape from his grasp, but he was too strong for her. Out of the corner of her eye, she saw Jerry suck in a deep gulp of air, then take a determined step forward.

Dee cried out as Jerry jumped onto the ghost man's back. Matthew Duncan groaned in pain and surprise. He fell forward onto the floor, letting go of Dee.

"Get off me!" he bellowed.

But Jerry didn't budge from his back. "Run, Dee," Jerry urged. "Go get help!"

Help? There was no one around, Dee remembered, standing frozen to the spot, staring down at Jerry and Matthew Duncan wrestling on the floor.

"Run!" Jerry yelled as the ghost rolled free, sprang to his feet, and grabbed Jerry around the waist.

"*No!*" Jerry cried, trying to break free.

"Wait!" Louisa's voice startled everyone. "It's me you want!" she yelled at the man, her eyes wild with fear and fury. "Leave the others alone and take me!"

Sensing his captor's confusion, Jerry tried to break away from him. When that failed, he swung back his foot and kicked his captor in the shin.

The man howled in pain, but didn't loosen his grip on Jerry.

"That—that hurt you," Dee stammered, confused.

"Of course it did," Jerry said proudly. "I kicked him really hard."

"But that means—" Dee began.

"He's *not* a ghost!" Louisa cried.

Before Matthew Duncan could reply, the door

to the room burst open. Eva ran in, followed by the gray-haired man she'd met at the clam bar.

"Stop right there, Duncan!" Eva cried as her companion pulled out his pistol.

Matthew Duncan's mouth dropped open. He quickly raised his hands high above his head.

"You're under arrest," Eva told him. She turned to her partner, who was holding up a badge so that everyone could see it. "Read him his rights, Stan."

Eva turned to Dee. "Are you all right? Did he hurt you or your friends?"

"No. We're okay," Dee said quietly. "Who is that man? Why is he here?" The questions started to pour out. "And who are you? I know you're not who you said you were."

"No, I'm sorry about that, Dee. I didn't want to lie, but I had to—because of my job."

"Your job?"

"I'm a detective with the downstate task force," she said. "My partner Stan and I have been after this man ever since he broke out of jail last December."

Dee's eyes widened with understanding. The fact that he was hiding out from the law explained a lot. That's why he'd been lurking around the abandoned guest house and why his complexion was so deathly pale. It even explained why he didn't have a decent jacket. You couldn't just walk into a store if you were afraid of being captured—even if you had enough money. And an escaped convict probably wouldn't have much money at all.

"We were able to put Mr. Duncan here in jail the first time for breaking and entering, but we could never prove he actually—"

"Excuse me," Louisa interrupted. "What is his name?"

"Matthew Duncan, or—like it says in his police file—Matthew Duncan the Fourth."

"Oh, my gosh!" Dee exclaimed softly. This wasn't the Matthew Duncan Louisa had known. This was some distant relative, perhaps his great-grandson! He wasn't a ghost and he never had been.

Eva gave Dee a curious look, then she turned back to her prisoner. "You're going back to the penitentiary, Duncan. And this time we'll prove you took the jewels."

"You can't prove anything," the man snarled as Stan handcuffed his hands behind his back. "I may get some more time for busting out, but that's it."

"You're wrong," Eva said. She stepped quickly past Jerry and Louisa, up to the wall where

Matthew Duncan had been chiseling at the plaster.

"There's nothing there," Matthew Duncan insisted.

"We'll see," Eva said quietly. She reached into the hole he had made in the wall and pulled out a long, narrow metal box. "I believe these are the jewels you—and we—were looking for," she said, a triumphant smile spreading across her face.

She opened the lid and held the box up for everyone to see. It was filled with jewelry—diamond necklaces, emerald earrings, ornate bracelets of silver and gold.

Matthew Duncan cursed and struggled to get away from Stan, but the gray-haired lawman held him firm.

"He stole these from the Dubois mansion here on the island two years ago," Eva explained.

"I know that house!" Louisa exclaimed. "It's been there ever since I—" At Dee's warning glance, she broke off abruptly. "It's very grand," she finished.

"Yes, it is," Eva agreed. "At the time, the only charges we could make stick were breaking and entering. He got a fairly light sentence." Turning to the scowling thief, she said, "You should have sat tight and done the time.

Your breaking out was all the excuse we needed to officially reopen this case.

"We knew you stole the jewels during the winter and that you stayed here at Winnifred's one night and at The Seagull Inn the next. Since the jewels were never found, we figured you'd hidden them either here or there. It was just a matter of time before you'd come back for them."

As Stan led Matthew Duncan away, Eva smiled at Dee, Jerry, and Louisa. "You kids were very brave."

"Thanks," said Dee.

Eva looked out into the hall. "I'd better go help Stan. We wouldn't want Duncan to slip away again. Besides, I left your poor father in the coffee shop waiting for me. That's where we were when Stan contacted me and said he'd followed Duncan into the inn."

"Does Dad know all about this?" Dee asked.

"No, and I want to tell him before he hears it anywhere else. In the future I'll never lie to him again. He's too nice a man."

*In the future?* Dee thought with a smile as Eva hurried from the room. She and her father apparently hadn't seen the last of Eva Barlow.

Dee looked to Louisa. "You're safe," she said. "It's all over."

Louisa appeared stunned with relief. She nodded her head slowly, as if letting the notion sink in. "Safe," she repeated softly.

"And we solved our mystery!" Jerry shouted happily.

"You were great!" said Dee. "I can't believe the way you jumped on that guy."

A small smile appeared on Jerry's face and quickly spread to a wide grin. "I did, didn't I?"

"You certainly did," Louisa agreed. "You were astonishingly brave!"

"Speaking of astonishing . . ." Jerry's happy face turned quizzical. "What was that you said about a ghost?"

"Oh, that," Louisa stalled, looking to Dee for help. "It was nothing. I was trying to get the man's attention away from you. I simply said the first thing that popped into my head."

Jerry shook his head solemnly. "I—I can't believe you would do something so risky for me," he told Louisa, looking down at the floor shyly. "No one has ever done anything like that for me before."

The three friends headed out of the room and down the stairs. Jerry said that he was feeling a little shaky from all the excitement and wanted to go home. "We'll walk you," Dee offered, feeling the need for some air herself.

They walked down the gravel path to the road. A warm breeze was blowing. There was no denying it, spring had finally arrived. As they walked, Dee wondered if bringing out the courageous side of Jerry was enough to give Louisa credit for helping him. How would they know if he was sufficiently helped?

Dee didn't have long to wonder. They turned a corner in the road and there, coming toward them, were Rob and Larry, the two boys who had bullied Jerry in school just the week before.

"If it isn't Merry Jerry and his two little girlfriends," Rob taunted.

# CHAPTER
## 20

"Uh-oh!" Dee said. "Come on, Jerry. Let's walk really fast."

"No way," Jerry said. "These punks don't scare me. I'd like to see them battle an escaped convict like I did."

He walked up boldly to the boys. "Why don't you two just shut your fat mouths and keep moving!" he told them.

"Haven't you had enough pain for one week?" Larry mocked him. He gave Jerry a shove, nearly sending him flying into Dee.

"You don't have to prove anything, Jerry," Louisa said, not wanting to see her friend beaten up again. "There are two of them, anyway."

"I can handle them," Jerry insisted, heading

back to the boys. He took a karate stance and kicked out at Larry. Laughing, the bully grabbed his leg and knocked him over backward.

Jerry got to his feet. "Oh, no. I'm afraid we've given him false confidence," Dee whispered to Louisa as Jerry confronted his tormentors again. When she didn't answer, Dee turned and looked at the empty space where Louisa had once been standing. "Louisa?"

But Dee had no time to worry about the ghost girl. Jerry had gotten back into his karate stance and was kicking wildly at the boys. With no trouble at all, they laughingly danced out of the way of his flying feet. Dee cringed. She couldn't bear to see Jerry humiliated yet again. And where in the world was Louisa?

Dee's eyes widened as Larry suddenly toppled over backward. It looked as if an invisible person had pulled his feet out from under him. Then Rob tripped forward just as mysteriously. Jerry hadn't seemed to touch him either.

At that moment a flatbed truck drove up and slowed to a stop. Nicky Dodge stuck his head out the window of the passenger side of his brother's pickup. "Does your friend need some help?" he asked Dee.

Dee wasn't sure. "I think he's actually han-

146

dling it himself," she said, not quite able to believe her eyes. "Thanks."

At the sound of Nicky's voice, the two bullies scrambled to their feet and ran back down the road. Jerry stood there, grinning happily. His body was a bit bruised, but his spirits were soaring. "I guess those guys won't mess with me again," he said. "And when they tell their friends about the new Jerry Mason, I think I'll be just fine."

"It looks like you definitely gave them something to talk about," Nicky said. "You guys need a lift?"

"I could use a ride home," said Jerry.

Nicky opened the cab door and Jerry climbed in. "Where's Louisa?" Jerry asked.

"Louisa!" In all the excitement, Dee had almost forgotten about her. "Louisa went to get help," she fibbed.

"Oh, well. You can tell her I won't be needing any more help," Jerry said. "But thank her anyway," he added, climbing up into the truck.

"I will," Dee assured him.

"Your aunt ordered some cod," Nicky said to Dee. "I told her I'd bring it up to the inn later. Will you be home?"

"Uh-huh," Dee said, feeling suddenly shy. Nicky Dodge really was good-looking. And nice, too!

"Then maybe I'll see you," Nicky said as his brother stepped on the gas.

Dee waved and then turned back up the road. Immediately, Louisa reappeared at her side. "I don't believe you!" Dee cried, giving her friend a hug. "You knocked those guys over, didn't you?"

Louisa smiled. "Jerry isn't the only one who has gotten braver." She laughed. "After this brush with Matthew Duncan the Fourth, I don't think I'll ever fear anything again." Louisa wrinkled her nose and laughed. "Not that it was altogether fair on my part. Being invisible can be quite an advantage."

"Once this gets around, I don't think anyone will bother with Jerry. Besides, with his new attitude, they wouldn't dare," said Dee.

Louisa suddenly stopped short and put her hand on her forehead.

"What's wrong?" Dee cried. "Are you all right?"

"The strangest thing," Louisa said dreamily. "For a fleeting moment, I just saw them—clear as day. Mother, Papa, and Edward. It was as if they were standing right beside me. So real I could almost touch them. And then they were gone."

"Louisa! Do you think that means that we've

helped Jerry? That you're one step closer to rejoining your family?"

"I'm sure of it," Louisa said slowly. "Somehow I know it in my heart." Her face glowed with happiness. "Oh, Dee. We did it. We really did it. We have only to find one more relative and I'll be back where I belong."

Dee hugged her. "We'll do it, Louisa. I promise we will."

"I believe you, Dee Forest," said Louisa. "I believe you can do anything. I wish I had known you all my life."

"It feels as if I *have* known you all my life," Dee replied, smiling fondly at Louisa. "It seems as if we've been friends forever."

The two girls started back to the inn. Above them, a flock of geese headed north. The sound of the waves crashed below. The sharpness of the ocean air mingled with the sweet smell of new green buds bursting forth. They didn't speak, but each was filled with a quiet happiness—the wordless connection that only true friends and soul mates ever know.

*Coming Soon:* **THE GHOST FERRY**

In book III of Haunting with Louisa, there's talk on Misty Island of a legendary ferry that comes to claim lost souls. So when Louisa disappears, Dee fears the worst! Here's a scene from *The Ghost Ferry*:

"Where are you, Louisa?" Dee cried out in frustration. Only the mournful sound of the foghorn answered her.

The tall pines behind Dee seemed to whisper as their needles rustled in the breeze. Again Dee had the feeling that she wasn't alone. Whoever—or whatever—had been in Mrs. Horace's parlor had followed her out. She was sure of it.

Rubbing the goose bumps from her arms, Dee summoned her courage. "Who are you?" she demanded bravely. "What do you want?"

Suddenly there was a loud snap. Dee's heart leapt into her throat as a low branch cracked behind her. She stood there a moment, straddling her bike, waiting for the spirit to appear, but everything remained quiet.

For the rest of the day, Dee couldn't shake the feeling that the presence was trailing her. But, because she didn't know what else to do, she kept looking for Louisa.

She went back to the graveyard and to the old Timmins mansion, which was now boarded up. She searched the old church on the far side of the island and even checked the high bluffs. There was no historic site on top of the bluffs, but Dee remembered Louisa telling her how she sometimes used to go there to look at the ocean and think.

Dee stood at the top of the bluffs and watched the waves crashing down on the rocky shore below. Around the bend she could see a rock jetty jutting out to sea. She realized that Fingers Cove was on the other side. She also remembered the small wooden cabin she and Louisa had discovered there. Mrs. Lockwood's son, William, had been living there when they found it early last fall. But he had since gone to live with his mother, and now it was empty.

*That would be a perfect place for a ghost to live,* Dee thought. Digging her feet into the sandy dirt, she began the difficult descent down the steep bluff. She had to hang on to the scrubby bushes to keep from falling. Even so, she slipped and took the last few feet of the bluff on her bottom. But finally, she was standing on the rocky beach.

Though it had been rough getting down, Dee knew it would be easier to walk along the shoreline to Fingers Cove than it would have been to bike there. The path into the cove was pitted with ditches and sprinkled with big rocks. She'd worry about getting back up the bluff later.

Dee stepped over driftwood and the remains of several damped-out campfires. Because of the weather, there were no swimmers or sunbathers in sight. Even in good weather not everyone wanted to hazard the descent down the bluff—or, for that matter, the difficult climb back up. The sea was rougher here and the shore much rockier than at the other beaches, so it was never exactly crowded. Today it seemed absolutely desolate.

A cold, wet drop plopped down on Dee's forehead. Another hit her cheek. The feeling of being followed persisted. "Who's there?" Dee cried. But again there was no response.

Dee stopped and covered her eyes with her hands. Maybe she was really losing her mind. There was no one there. She was talking to herself like a crazy person.

She sat down on a rock. What if her mother's death had really unhinged her? What if Louisa didn't even exist? Maybe she'd imagined the whole thing. A shiver ran up Dee's spine. What if this whole winter she'd been hanging out with a figment of her own imagination?

Dee shook off that thought. Louisa might be a ghost, but she was real enough. And now she might be in terrible trouble. Dee *had* to find her.

She continued along the shoreline, jumping from rock to rock. The seawater splashed up and ran under her feet. That and the rain, which was falling harder and harder, made the rocks extremely slippery. More than once, she almost lost her footing.

Finally she turned another bend in the shoreline and came to Fingers Cove. Here the rocks gave way to a bed of soft sand, rimmed by a dense pine forest. The rain was falling steadily now. It was hard for Dee to gauge the time because of the fog, but she guessed it was almost seven in the evening. She'd spent hours searching for Louisa.

Dee realized she'd be in trouble when she got back to the inn. She had forgotten about helping with the breakfast dishes, and she hadn't told anyone where she was going. She would just check this one last spot, she told herself, then she'd head back and face the music.

The beach was deserted and no one was out on the rocky jetties, the fingerlike protrusions that gave the place its name. "Louisa?" she called. Nothing. But as Dee turned toward the forest where the cabin was, she caught sight of something in the water.

Hovering at the end of the jetty, Dee could just make out the murky form of a squarish boat. Its outline wavered in the mist. The boat rose and fell, buffeted by the waves that lapped against the jetty.

Dee peered through the fog. The boat was old. She'd never seen one like it down at the harbor or the marina. And there was no reason for a boat to be anchored over here. It didn't make sense. Unless . . .

"The ghost ferry!" Dee gasped.


*Could Louisa be on that ferry? If not, where is she? Will Dee ever see Louisa again?*

## ABOUT THE AUTHOR

EMILY CATES was born in New York City but she spent her summers on the coast of Maine, which gave her the inspiration for the Haunting with Louisa trilogy. She has written several books for adults and has published poetry in several journals. *The Ghost in the Attic*, the first book in the Haunting with Louisa trilogy, was her first book for young readers. *The Mystery of Misty Island Inn* is her second, and is the second in the trilogy. Ms. Cates now divides her time between Boston, Massachusetts, and Block Island, Rhode Island, which is very much like Misty Island.

# Magical Skylark Adventures!